CRUISE BULLY

BY

LAWRENCE W. BAXTER

Cruise Bully by Lawrence W. Baxter

The grandparents take four of their grandkids on an unforgettable Caribbean Cruise. The grandkids work together when faced with some unexpected experiences.

Zander has to fight an army brat bully who's a head taller and 2 years older;

Garret must solve the most difficult scavenger hunt ever;

Lexi faces an obnoxious room steward and finds a love interest;

Talin is tormented by an overweight adult and becomes BFF with a girl from France.

INDEX		Page

Prologue		5
Day 1		
Chapter 1	Airplane Ride	8
Chapter 2	Cruise Terminal	11
Chapter 3	Staterooms	17
Chapter 4	Safety Drill	20
Chapter 5	First Night	27
Chapter 6	Scavenger Hunt	30
Chapter 7	Dinner	34
Chapter 8	Deck Party	38
Day 2		
Chapter 9	Day at Sea	41
Chapter 10	Pool Area	45
Chapter 11	Magic Show	49
Day 3		
Chapter 12	Cayman Island	51
Chapter 13	Stingray City	56
Chapter 14	Game Room	60
Chapter 15	Captain's Table	63
Chapter 16	Exercise Room	66
Chapter 17	Tank Rescue	69
Chapter 18	Teen Club	73

Day 4

Chapter 19   Amber Cove   78

Chapter 20   Art Gallery   82

Chapter 21   Casino   87

Chapter 22   The Robbery   92

Day 5

Chapter 23   La Romana   95

Chapter 24   Shops   99

Chapter 25   The Rosary   102

Chapter 26   Zander has a Date 105

Chapter 27   The Showdown   109

Chapter 28   The Rescue   113

Chapter 29   The Reward   118

Day 6

Chapter 30   Ship Tour   121

Chapter 31   Medical Center   124

Chapter 32   Outdoor Movie   128

Day 7

PROLOGUE

FORT DIX, NEW JERSEY

There was yelling in the kitchen but neither Burt nor his brother Brian in their bedroom could hear all that was being said. But they did hear their father yell, **"Since when does a kid have to repeat his freshmen year in high school! Going on this cruise takes him out of school. If he's flunking, he should be in school."**

Then they hear their mother, **"I know, but it's my parent's 50th wedding anniversary celebration. My sister's family will be there from France and my brother is coming from California. The boys hardly ever get to see them. You promised that you would go."**

There's more conversation, but they can't hear it. Then they hear the outside door slam and a little later mom comes into their room. Her eyes are red and she is dabbing them with a Kleenex.

"So, what's going on?" Brian asks.

"Your dad isn't going on the cruise with us. He's going to sign up for another tour in the Middle East."

"But haven't grandpa and grandma already paid for his ticket for the cruise?"

Yes, but you know your father. Principles before money."

Burt now asks, "Why isn't he going? It's because of me isn't it?"

Mom is silent for awhile, trying to choose her words.

"Burt, you know the counselor wants you to repeat your freshman year. I'm in favor of it but your dad is strongly against it. I know that you don't want to either, so you get your wish."

"We leave for the airport early in the morning. Will I get to see dad before we leave?" Burt asks.

"I don't know, Burt...I don't know."

Mom leaves the room.

In the silence that follows, Burt is upset. He was looking forward to a week on the cruise with his dad. The last conversation he had with his dad wasn't good. Dad had criticized him for starting a fight at school. "Let the other guy start it, you dummy." he had said. "Then you won't get into trouble."

Burt knew his father was talking from experience. Dad dropped out of high school after his junior year. He went into the army and with bravado rose in the ranks to sergeant. "Being the toughest and strongest is all you need to get ahead," he always said.

Even with his dad gone overseas a lot, Burt admired his father and wanted to follow in his footsteps. Out loud, Burt says, "I'm going to kick ass with every boy that's on the cruise."

Brian, age ten and four years younger than Burt, becomes a little worried, "What are you going to do with me?"

"Brian, you're safe. You're smart, popular and probably going to college. You're my brother and you put up with me. I also like that you don't tell on me."

Chapter 1 Airplane Ride

DAY 1

The adventure begins on an airline flight out of the Midway Airport, Chicago to Fort Lauderdale, Florida. While the two sets of parents and grandma are seated in the back of the plane, the cabin steward puts the four grandkids and grandpa in the first row which she claims is a special row. There are three seats on each side of the aisle. On one side is 12 year old Garret, dressed in his favorite color, green. He sits next to the window. His cousin, Lexi, age 10 and with long blond hair almost always in a ponytail is in the middle seat. Grandpa is next to the aisle.

On the other side, Garret's brother, Zander, the oldest grandchild and in eighth grade is in the aisle seat. His cousin, Talin, who is Lexi's sister and the youngest grandchild at age nine, is in the middle. Next to the window is a giant of a man. He is so big; the armrest between him and Talin can't be lowered. The flight attendant brings him an extension for his seatbelt.

He's in the first row because there's more leg room. It's the only row on the plane he can fit into. So the smallest person on the plane, Talin, is placed next to the biggest person on the plane. He just looks out the window.

This doesn't go well for Talin. For one thing she can't see out the window because his bulk blocks her view. For another, she can't use all of her seat. The big guy's butt takes half of her seat. Talin who's afraid of bugs and germs doesn't want to touch him, so she moves away.

"Talin, give me some room," says Zander.

Talin in a whispering voice replies, "I can't; look at the 'whale' next to me."

"Oh," says Zander while adjusting his head phones, "guess you can't help it."

"Also," replies Talin, still in a whisper, "he's making me uncomfortable. I can't see out the window and look; he's got Cheeto crumbs all down the front of him. UGH!"

The big guy stirs, turns to look down at Talin and asks, "What's your name little lady?"

Talin wonders why if calling someone big, fat or a whale is impolite, why isn't calling me little just as bad? Talin tells him her name.

"Well, that's a nice name, little lady. My name is Tank,"

There's that word 'little' again, thinks Talin. Talin looks at him in disbelief. He has a two-inch beard, bushy eyebrows and longest nose hair she has ever seen. All the hair has a red hue to it. He's wearing what appears to be a sweat suit. Talin takes care in what she wears, always trying to look fashionable.

He continues in soft, pleasant voice, "Just kidding. Tank is what my friends call me. My real name is Erwin, so you can see why I don't mind the nickname. And it's better than all the terrible names fat people get called, like WHALE." Tank then turns and stares out the window.

He heard me, thinks Talin. He's upset with me and I've got to ride on this plane next to him for TWO

HOURS! This plane ride will be horrible! Talin is sulking. She wants to twirl her hair with her fingers, but doesn't. It's a habit she is trying to break.

The flight attendant gives the safety instructions. When she gets to the part that we can use our seat cushion as a life vest in the event of a crash into the ocean, Zander quips, "In the event we are crashing, I'll use my seat cushion as a toilet." The attendant gives him a smile and continues on with her safety talk. The rest of us try to control our laughter.

The plane takes off and Garret and Lexi watch out their window. It is a clear day with few clouds so they can see the ground for a long time. A little while into the flight, the pilot announces we will be cruising at 583 mph, at an altitude of 28,000 feet and we can turn on our electronics.

Grandpa googles the plane, which is a Boeing 737. He announces it seats 137 passengers, costs 60 million dollars to build and that over 9,700 of these planes have been built. The grandkids are hardly interested. Garret, a year younger than his brother Zander, pulls out a hand puzzle. Lexi is reading a book and Zander is listening to music through his headphones. Talin feels squashed and resists the urge to twirl her hair. Tank is eating trail mix and she can hear him chewing. Can this get any worse?

The flight attendant appears with a tray in her hands. She asks Zander if he would like a snack. Zander replies, "What are my choices?"

"Yes or no," she answers, then smiles and winks at him. This must be payback for his joke. She gives him a bag of peanuts.

Talin passes a bag of peanuts to Tank who thanks her and apologies for taking up so much room. Instead of eating the peanuts, he puts them away, gets out an Ipad and says, "I'm a gamer. Are you?"

"What's a gamer?" Talin asks.

"It's somebody who spends too much time playing video games. I hope you don't do that."

Talin doesn't feel like carrying on a conversation with Tank and just responds with a quick, "I don't." She then turns her head and starts a conversation with Zander. "What are you listening to?"

Zander takes off his head phones and answers, "Shock wave and I'd like to listen to them. Anything else?"

Talin is troubled. *Zander doesn't want to be bothered and I don't want to talk to the whale. I want to play on my Ipad, but I just told him I don't play much.*

Talin pulls the airline magazine out of the seat pocket in front of her. There's a lot of advertisements and articles showing beautiful people and places. *Nothing I want to read.* However the page showing the world and all the places to where the airplane flies is interesting.

After awhile, Tank puts away his Ipad and appears to go to sleep.

Talin uses this as an opportunity to play a game on her Ipad.

Talin is now sure Tank is sleeping. Just for something to do more than need, she goes to the bathroom and upon returning says to Zander, "What if he (nodding towards Tank) needs to go to the bathroom? I was just there and there's no way he can even get through the door."

"I can explain that little lady." Tank says, scaring Talin because she thought he was asleep. Also there's the use of that word 'little' again in describing her. "We big people avoid the problem by not drinking anything hours before our flight or on the flight. However, just to be safe, I wear a giant diaper and guess what?"

"What?" asks Talin.

"I peed too while you were in the bathroom."

"EWWW" cries Talin, "Somebody change seats with me. I can't take this anymore!" She tries to stand up, but Tank gently pushes her back down and says, "Just kidding little lady. I didn't pee and I'm not wearing a diaper. Just funning you."

"Not funny," says Talin in a disgusting way and she twirls her hair. She is totally freaked. Tank goes back to playing a video game.

A little later, Tank asks, "Talin, I need you to do me a favor."

"What?"

"My feet are swelling. I need to take my shoes off. I can't do it myself while in this seat. Would you mind?"

OMG, Talin is thinking, *how do I get out of this?* She looks down at his feet. They are slip ons, so this may not be so bad.

Talin gets down on the floor and struggles removing Tank's shoes. He laughs at her efforts. They are not only huge but heavy. They also smell. She doesn't say a word.

"Thank you, Talin, that's a relief."

Good for you, thinks Talin. *I look forward to putting them back on you when we land. Not.*

Chapter 2 Cruise Terminal

After the plane ride and collecting luggage, it's a shuttle bus ride from the airport to the cruise terminal. The cruise terminal is a large two story building on a big dock. Tied to the dock with enormous ropes is the largest ship the grandkids have ever seen. It is as long as four football fields, 11 stories tall, carries 2000 passengers and 1150 crew members. It is taller than any buildings in the towns where the grandkids are from. 'Awesome' the grandkids say.

There is a long line of people waiting to go onto the ship. There aren't any other kids that might be in the grandkids' age group. This is due to school being in session. Our family is here for several reasons. It was the only week all the parents could get off from their respective jobs at the same time and it wasn't a black out period for using the reward points on the grandparents' credit card. Besides, grandma is a retired grade school teacher and can work with the kids on their school work. Which is why the grandkids brought assignments to do while they are out of school.

The long lines for the check-in counters snake back and forth six times. Even though there are perhaps 30 counter workers checking people in; it is a slow process.

The grandkids are very active. They have been sitting for a two-hour plane ride and a 30-minute shuttle ride from the airport. They have a lot of pent up energy. All four are trying to stand and walk on their hands. They let the line of people in front of them move far enough ahead so there is space for cartwheels. People laugh at them.

Talin attempts a back flip, loses her balance and goes tumbling two lines over and lands against … a big, giant of a man. It is Tank! Talin freezes.

Tank gently picks her up and says, "Well little lady, we meet again."

"I'M NOT A LITTLE LADY!" Talin hollers, "STOP CALLING ME THAT."

"And I'm not a whale, okay?" replies Tank. "Okay," Talin replies meekly. "I'm sorry." while thinking to herself that he really is a whale.

Talin walks back all disgusted and embarrassed. She twirls her hair and stands silently in line. The other grandkids also stand quietly in sympathy for her. They all keep peeking back at Tank. He smiles back in return.

Finally at the counter, tickets and identification are presented. The counter person holds a small camera and takes a picture of each person for use on a Ship and Sail credit card. This Ship and Sail card will double as a room key and a type of credit card to buy anything on the ship. Garret tries to ham it up for his picture. He stretches his mouth with his fingers, but the counter lady sees him do it. So he has to pose again. Lexi and Zander also try making a funny face, but each is caught.

However, when it is Talin's turn, she gets away with it. The counter lady is distracted by a coworker. She doesn't notice Talin removing her glasses and raising her upper lip. Talin's picture hardly looks like Talin. The cards are issued. Talin is proud of hers. She got away with something the others didn't.

After the counter check in, it's a walk out to the pier and then onto an enclosed gangplank into the ship. There are some workmen working on the side of the ship near the water line. Sparks are flying, meaning they are doing some welding. Upon entering the ship, there is a band playing, waiters handing out drinks and pictures being taken. It is a festive affair.

An elevator takes us to the fifth floor. When the doors open, we step into a large beautifully decorated room. The ceiling is 6 floors high. Every level has a balcony with a brass railing surrounding it.

"This is called the atrium," grandpa announces while everybody takes in the splendor of the scene.

"What's an atrium?" Lexi asks while looking up.

Grandpa answers, "It's a large room in the middle of a hotel with a high ceiling."

"But we're not in a hotel."

This time Lexi's mother answers, "Yes we are.... It's a hotel on the water. A floating five star hotel!" One can tell she is impressed.

The next task is finding the five staterooms which will be home for the next six days.

Chapter 3 Staterooms

The staterooms are on deck 10. There are three Oceanside staterooms with outside balconies on the water for the parents and grandparents. Across the hallway are two interior rooms with no windows for the grandkids. One for the boys and one for the girls.

Waiting at the staterooms, is a short, brown-skinned man with thick but short black hair who says, "Hola, estoy Diego y enfermo ser tu habitacion mayordomo."

Lexi immediately recognizes the language but not what he said. "We're not Spanish. We're American," Lexi says.

The man replies angrily in English and looking directly at Lexi, "I'm American, too. I'm from Chile which is in South America, so we're all Americans. Not just you people from the United States. I get tired of you people thinking you are the only Americans on the continents of North and South America!" He was almost shouting.

Wow, thinks Zander, *this guy has a problem. He's calling us 'you people'.*

"Sorry, we're not used to being around foreigners," Lexi says.

"Foreigners, I not a foreigner. This my ship and on it you are the foreigners." Then looking at the 4 grandkids he says in a calmer voice, "I am your room steward and my name is Diego. I take care of you, clean your room, make your bed, change your towels, keep secrets you want me to keep from your parents. (He glances and winks at the adults.) Anything you need, I get for you. I'm 44 years old and the best job I can get is waiting on you rich kids. I don't like it, but I do my job. Comprehendo?"

The kids are stunned and stand quietly, wondering what happens next.

Diego snatches Lexi's Ship and Sail card and says, "I show you how to use key. Your luggage is in your rooms. Anything you need or questions, call me; the number on desk in your rooms. Do not give me trouble and no damage anything in your rooms. We good?"

"Yeah, we're good," replies Zander, still stunned by Diego's attitude and thinking we kids didn't ask for a 44-year-old servant from Chile. He made his choice; why take it out on us.

While Diego demonstrates how to use the card as a door key, he says that on the previous cruise, he had four kids on his floor that caused him a lot of trouble and did some damage to their rooms. His boss blamed him and Diego just wants to make sure it doesn't happen again.

"We understand," says grandpa, "and we'll make sure you don't have trouble from these kids."

"Gracias," replies Diego and he leaves to greet other passengers (foreigners according to him) coming onto his floor.

The sisters and brothers enter their respective staterooms. They are like a hotel room but smaller. Each has two single beds and a couch. There is a small table in front of the couch facing a wall-mounted TV above a desk with a mirror. There are two closets, a few drawers and a small bathroom with sink, toilet and shower. On the sink are soap, shampoo, conditioner, body lotion and drinking glasses wrapped in plastic. The kids think the rooms are okay except there isn't much floor space for their clothes.

The first thing they do is recharge their electronic devices. They discover there's only 1 outlet at the desk. Another outlet is discovered at the top of the bathroom mirror which they can't reach without climbing on the sink. Forget about calling Diego. They climb the sink.

Next is unpacking the clothes. Talin can't reach the clothes bar in the closet and Lexi has to hang her dresses for her. After unpacking, an announcement comes over the intercom.

"ALL PASSENGERS REPORT TO THEIR MUSTER STATIONS ON THE LIFEBOAT DECK WITH THEIR LIFEJACKETS WHICH ARE IN A DRAWER UNDER THE COUCH.

Chapter 4 Safety Drill

"OMG, WE'RE SINKING" Talin shouts.

"We're not sinking. We haven't even left the port Talin." Lexi says, "I bet it's a safety drill. Come on, let's go in the hallway and find the others."

In the hallway grandpa tells the kids that everybody is to go to deck 5 and not to use the elevators. The instructions are on the back side of the room door.

"Is it just a drill?" asks Talin, trying to remain calm.

"Yes," her dad replies. "Follow me."

He leads the way down the stairs from deck 10. Other passengers are going down the stairs, too. At deck 7, the stairs are getting crowded. In the mix are two boys and a girl who wears black rimmed glasses with straight black hair and looks Talin's age. Another message comes from the intercom. *"ALL PASSENGERS REPORT TO DECK 5 WITH THEIR LIFE JACKETS IMMEDIATELY."*

One of the other boys says to his friend, "I heard that the welders working on the boat caused an explosion which created a large hole in the side of the boat."

The other boy responds, "Yeah, I heard what sounded like an explosion and they don't think they can fix it. We're probably going to sink before we even get out of the port."

This freaks Talin, but she doesn't say anything. She remembers seeing the welders. The crowd of passengers moves slowly, now reaching deck 6. The unknown boys continue talking.

"I heard of a cruise ship somewhere in Europe that sank before it got out of port. It was horrible and some people died."

"Yeah, because it was in port they couldn't lower the lifeboats and they had already removed the gangplank. The tilt of the boat prevented the crew from putting the gangplank back."

"Hurry, hurry!" Talin says to no one in particular and she starts pushing Garret who is ahead of her.

"Stop it," says Garret.

"But we're sinking."

Garret, "We're not sinking; we're in port."

Talin, "Ships can sink in port, I heard it has happened."

The two older boys laugh, enjoying the panic they are causing for Talin. Now at deck 5, the intercom blares again: *PLEASE CONTINUE TO YOUR MUSTER STATION. INSTRUCTIONS WILL BE GIVEN AT YOUR MUSTER STATION.*

Talin is now looking for running room.

At deck 5, a crew member is telling people where their muster station is. She tells people from decks 10 and 7 to go to muster station 'D'. At muster station 'D' the passengers are standing like they are in a fire drill formation. The two other strange boys and the girl are next to our group. The two boys continue talking about the sinking of our ship.

Talin says to Zander, "Hear that; this is not a drill, we are sinking."

"We are not sinking; these guys are having fun scaring you," says Zander.

"You calling me a liar?" says the larger of the two boys who overhears Zander. He has a military-style short haircut, broad shoulders and is a head taller than Zander.

"We aren't sinking," was all Zander could think of saying.

"Whether we're sinking or not, I say you called me a liar. Are you going to deny that too?"

"I didn't call you a liar."

"I say you did." and the boy bumps his chest into Zander.

Zander thinks this is weird. This kid obviously wants a fight, but he wouldn't start it with the parents nearby, would he? So Zander tries a friendly approach and says, "My name is Zander, what's yours?"

"What's it to you? Before this cruise is over you and I are going to have it out. We're on a ship so you can't get away." The boy is not only talking smack but looking mean. He could be trouble.

Before Zander can respond, a crew member tells everyone to be quiet. She explains the procedure in case of an emergency. What she says about the lifeboats is the most interesting.

"Each lifeboat is fully enclosed so you will be protected from the cold or rain. The orange color of the lifeboat is so it can be easily seen by rescue ships. Each boat has oars, flares, mirrors for signaling, first aid supplies, food and water. There's a marine radio, heater, and extra fuel for the motor. There's even a sail in case the engine doesn't work. Any questions?"

The girl with the black rimmed glasses asks, "How many people can fit into a lifeboat?" *Good question,* thinks Talin.

"150" the crew member answers.

"And how many lifeboats are there?" *Another good question,* thinks Talin.

"18" replies the crew member.

Talin couldn't multiply the numbers, so she asks Zander, "How many people would that be?"

The girl with the glasses overhears and answers "2700, but that's not enough for 2000 passengers and 1150 crew members which totals 3150 people."

Just then the older boy, who had challenged Zander, says. "That leaves out you people on deck 10, the farthest from the lifeboats. We're on deck 7, so we'll get to the lifeboats first. You'll go down with the ship."

Talin is scared again. The crew member continues on, "In case any of you did the calculation, you know we don't have enough lifeboats for everybody. In large canisters on deck 3 are a dozen blow up rafts. Each of these rafts can hold up to 50 people. The passengers get the lifeboats with at least 1 crew member to operate it. The crew members use the life rafts. So there's more than enough room for everyone on the ship. Now if there are no more questions, everyone can go back to their rooms."

On the way back up the stairs, the two other boys stay close. They ask Zander who his friends are. Zander introduces Garret as his brother and his cousins, Talin and Lexi.

Looking straight into Garret's eyes, the taller boy who looks around age 15, asks, "What room you in?"

"1012" Garret immediately replies and the tall boy continues staring, smiles and stays silent.

"What are your names?" asks Garret.

As the ship's horn goes off singling we are leaving port, the taller one says, "My name is Burdette, but everyone calls me Burt."

Garret then makes a grave mistake. Due to the ship's horn, Garret doesn't hear clearly and says laughingly, "Did you say Butt? You're called Butt?"

"No smart ass; you call me Burt. Also understand my brother and I are army brats and I know many forms of martial arts. I'll let you get away this once. Next time you make a mistake like that with me, you'll regret it!"

Good grief thinks Garret, and he stays silent.

Breaking the silence, the other boy says he's Burt's younger brother and he introduces himself as Brian. He seems carefree, a lot nicer and appears to be about 10 years old. He's tall and thin and acts in an easy going style. Brian introduces his cousin who is the girl with the black rimmed glasses much like Talin wears, "Her name is Bernadette but we call her Bernie. She's from France."

"She's the smart one in our family." adds Brian. Bernie is embarrassed. She starts twirling her hair. She is about the same size as Talin and is wearing something that looks like a Girl Scout uniform. Talin immediately likes her.

Brian continues on, proving he is indeed nicer than his older brother, "Bernie's parents are both college professors. That's where she gets her smarts from. We're here as part of a family celebration. It's our grandparent's 50th wedding anniversary and they're paying for everything. However my dad couldn't make it, he's in the army and …"

"Don't tell'm Brian, that's classified information," Burt interrupts.

"No it's not." Brian replies.

"Yes it is for these clowns. They look like spies to me," says Burt and adds looking at Zander and Garret, "And you know what we do with spies? We beat the crap out of them!"

At deck 7 Burt, Brian and Bernadette ("Bernie") leave and head to their staterooms. "See you around Zander," Burt says with a sneer as he departs. Zander feels this is a threat. Then Burt looks back and adds, "You too, Garret."

Now Garret feels threatened and asks, "Why me; what did I do?"

"You called me a butt."

"It was an accident. I couldn't hear. The ship's horn was going off."

Burt and Brian just keep on walking without responding.

"Wow, that kid is a dork," Lexi says continuing up the stairs to deck 10.

Chapter 5 First Night

The grandkids go to their parents rooms which have balconies to watch as the ship lumbers out of port. Being on deck 10 has the advantage of being able to see over the city of Fort Lauderdale. The ship picks up speed. Farther out, the waves and swales get higher and the wind increases. It's an awesome experience. Soon the view is nothing but ocean spread across the bottom of the horizon.

The grandkids want to go swimming, but the swimming pools are empty. Overnight, seawater will be pumped into the pools. They have to wait until tomorrow to go swimming. Grandpa offers to take everybody on a tour of the boat. The parents decline. They are tired from the travel day and want to relax and get dressed for dinner.

So off goes grandpa with his four grandkids. They locate the spa with a beauty salon, casino, game center, gift shop and a teenage nightclub. There are several specialty restaurants, one offering ice cream, and the others either pizza or hamburgers. There's even a sushi bar. There is a buffet restaurant and two main dining rooms. They see the Atrium Lounge again and notice that it has a dance floor, bar and a stage for entertainment. A band is playing Motown music, but the kids aren't interested. There are three banks of elevators in the front, middle and rear sections of the boat.

Outside on the promenade deck, the deck on which you can walk around the outside of the boat, Garret and Talin say they are ready to go back.

"This is getting confusing." said Lexi, "I don't know which way to go. Where are we?"

"We're on the port side of the ship," says grandpa, "When you are facing toward the front of the ship, which is called the bow, left is port and right is starboard. Left is a shorter word than right and port is a shorter word than starboard. That's how you can remember port is on the left side and starboard is on the right side. The back of the boat is called either aft or stern."

While passing through the Atrium, grandpa goes to get a drink at the bar to take back to the room. While he's away, the grandkids have a discussion.

Zander, "What are we going to about Burt and Brian? They're bullies."

"Not Brian," objects Lexi, "I thought he was nice."

"Let's call them B & B." suggests Garrett, trying to make fun of them. Then he adds, "Since the girl's name also begins with a B, we can call them the 3 Bs."

"I don't think it was smart for you to tell them our room number," says Zander.

"Sorry, just trying to be nice. At least we know they are on deck 7 and we can avoid that one." says Garret, and then adds, "What did they mean when they said they were army brats?"

When grandpa returns, Zander asks, "Grandpa, you were in the army. What is an army brat?"

"An army brat is a kid whose parent or parents are in the army. They live on a military base and go to school on the base. An army brat is different because the families have to relocate almost every two years. Therefore the kids are in a new school with every transfer, including going overseas if the parent is sent there. So there's little stability while they are growing up. Any friends they make are temporary because they have to relocate so often. They may develop problems getting along with other kids. Sometimes the parent who is in the military is gone for long periods of time. For example, Navy deployments on a ship may last eight months....."

"Okay, okay, grandpa, I get it." interrupts Zander.

"Why do you ask?"

"No reason, just wondering." The grandkids are wondering what life on the ship is going to be like with Burt around. They walk in silence back to their rooms.

Chapter 6 Scavenger Hunt

Back in their rooms, the parents tell the kids to get ready for dinner and to dress up. Lexi and Talin get into dresses. Zander and Garret are mystified by a note that is under their door. The note with a 1 inside a circle says: '*HARRY POTTER/DINGES*'.

While thinking about the note they put on button-down shirts and dockers. Garret's clothes are green.

Garret, "What does this mean?"

Zander, "I don't know … and who put it there?"

While they are pondering the message, the girls come into their room and the boys show the note to them.

"I know who Harry Potter is. I read the book," says Lexi.

"Yes, we know about Harry Potter, but what does Dinges mean? And what's the point of the note?"

The kids show the note to their parents, but the parents know nothing about it.

"Let's go to dinner." the parents say. Grandpa leads the way to the dining room. He asks the kids, "How do you like the cruise so far?"

The response is a polite, "Great, grandpa," but the reality is they are not really pleased with their first day on the cruise:

Zander and Garret because of the exchange they had with Burt.

Talin keeps glancing around for Tank. He's a creep in her mind.

Lexi is upset with the run-in she had with Diego, the room steward.

Now there's an unexplained note that doesn't make any sense. What's going on?

There's a long line of people waiting to enter the dining room. The waiting line is adjacent to the library on the ship. While standing there, Lexi reads a memorial plaque on the wall next to the library entrance door.

Suddenly she exclaims to the kids, "Follow me, follow me!" and hurries into the library. The kids follow her and Lexi starts examining the book titles on the shelves.

"What are you doing?"

"Find the Harry Potter book!" Lexi responds and frantically moves from shelf to shelf.

"Why?"

"The plaque outside next to the door says this is the Dinges Library!"

"Way to go, Lexi," and everybody searches for a Harry Potter book.

"Here it is," says Garret and as he opens it, a bookmark falls to the floor. Everybody takes turns examining the book but nothing looks unusual. The book mark however has lines and dots on it.

"It's got to be the book mark," says Lexi.

"Why," replies Zander, "it's just lines and dots."

"There's also a number 2 in a circle at the bottom. Didn't the note under your door have a 1 in a circle on it?"

"Yes it is did, so?"

"So they're connected. I bet it's a scavenger hunt," Lexi says excitedly, "The note is clue number 1 and this is clue number 2."

Garret, "But this clue is nothing but lines and dots. How could it mean anything?"

"We didn't think the note Harry Potter/Dinges meant anything either. But now we know," Lexi replies.

"Let's ask grandpa," Garret suggest, "he's always doing scavenger hunts for us."

The kids get back in line for the dining room. It's taking awhile to get a round table that seats 10 for everybody. The kids show and ask grandpa about the bookmark. He has no idea and they get the same answer from grandma and their parents.

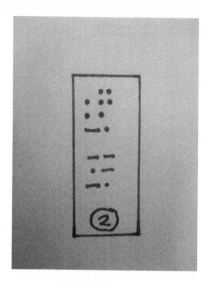

Chapter 7 Dinner

A large round table for 10 on a raised platform in the center of a beautiful dining room finally becomes available. A maître de in a suit, white shirt and tie leads the way to the table. He pulls chairs out for grandma and the mothers. Lexi is already in her seat, but Talin stands waiting for her turn to be seated. She gets treated the same as the older women and says, "Thank you sir."

"Enjoy," says the maître de and he leaves. A waiter then takes the white cloth napkins, unfolds and places them in each person's lap. Except Lexi who has already done hers. The table is covered with a white tablecloth and has an ice sculpture of a dolphin in the middle. The chairs have red velvet seats and backs. There are several large vases with flowers on pedestals spread around the dining room.

Square columns with mirrors on the sides define the aisles through which waiters and waitresses in white jackets and black pants are hustling back and forth. Each has a small white cloth draped over their left arm. There are more utensils than the kids know what to do with. The silverware, plates and glasses are first class.

"Glad I dressed up," says Lexi.

"Me too," says Talin acting like a princess with her hands in her lap. Zander and Garret already have elbows on the table. Grandpa points out the large chandeliers hanging from the ceiling.

As a waiter fills the glasses with water, he apologizes for the long wait and says we can get in quicker by requesting smaller tables. The adults decide from now on to request a table of six for the adults and a nearby table of four for the grandkids. The grandkids are delighted with that news.

Grandpa asks the waiter where he is from. "The Philippines." He replies. "In fact; most of the wait staff in this restaurant are from the Philippines. We work six months straight on the ship and then have two months off."

"At least he's not from Chile," Lexi says to the kids who laugh at her comment.

"Oh, you must have met Diego," says the waiter.

"How would you know that?" Grandpa asks.

"Diego is the only one on the ship from Chile. He's one of a kind. But really, he's very nice. All bark no bite. He's been on cruise ships longer than most of us."

The waiter continues talking about his job and schedule, but the grandkids aren't interested.

They are looking around the room for Burt. They don't see him. *Great,* thinks Zander; *I can enjoy dinner in peace.*

The menus are delivered and the grandkids are disappointed. There are no choices for pizza, burgers or chicken fingers.

For the first course, the choices are wedge salad, lobster soup or smoked moulard duck breast. The kids pass on the first course and eat the rolls instead. The main course is not any better. They skip the crab cakes, salmon, and Greek zucchini fritters. The boys go with the braised beef short ribs and the girls order the glazed chicken breast.

During dinner, a waiter from another area on the restaurant with a 'Don' name tag brings Talin a green-colored slushy drink. He says, "It's a green slime smoothie. Compliments of a secret admirer."

"Who?" asks Talin.

"Not supposed to tell you." replies the waiter.

Everybody starts kidding her about having a secret admirer. Talin scans the room and sees Tank by the windows at a table for four. He's alone on one side and there's a man and women across from him. Grandpa explains that the big guy is the one Talin helped with his shoes on the plane.

Talin takes a taste, makes a face and asks "What's in it?"

The waiter replies, "two cups strawberries, 1 banana, honey and …." The waiter hesitates….

"And what?" Talin insists.

"two cups spinach." finishes the waiter.

The description of the drink doesn't sound good to Talin either. She tastes it again, makes another disgusting face and then concludes it's bad.

The dessert choices are more to the kids' liking. Each orders a different one. They are: strawberry cheesecake, cinnamon spiced apples, caramel cake and vanilla ice cream with blackberry sauce.

Table discussion revolves around what to do after dinner. Also, can the grandkids wander about the ship without an adult? The men think it's OK, but the women think an adult should be with them at least for the first night.

Zander and Garrett are thinking they don't want to go anywhere alone where Burt might be. Grandpa says there's a welcome aboard party on deck 9 with a DJ that might be good. Everybody agrees that is a good idea. Zander and Garrett are relieved. Burt certainly wouldn't try anything if the parents are along.

After dinner it's back to the rooms. The kids immediately check I pads or cell phones. Garret hollers, "There's no Internet," and followed by Zander, runs to his parents' room.

"Garret, we are out in the middle of the ocean. There are no cell towers out here, so there's no Internet. It costs $15.00 a day for each of us to hook onto the ship's Wi-Fi and grandpa elected not to pay for that," his dad answers, "Only grandma has internet access."

"But I can't check my e-mail or play games." say the boys.

"We are on vacation." the parents explain. "You'll have to get along without the Internet for a while. You may be able to get on the Internet the next time we're in port."

"But that's not for two days," the boys complain and go back to their rooms having had another unpleasant cruise experience.

Chapter 8 Deck Party

On deck 9, the deck party is already going. Deck 10 above it is a partial deck and they stand at a railing overlooking the people dancing and drinking below. There's loud music the kids like and they are given glow sticks.

Zander carefully scans the crowd and there's no sign of Burt. Zander can relax. The adults get drinks and the kids, soda and popcorn. The social director conducts a few adult games which are fun to watch. Then karaoke starts with some participants pretty good but most are off key.

After karaoke, a band plays and Garret, Lexi and Talin dance to the music. Zander keeps watching the crowd of passengers below. He spots Brain and Burt with their mother come onto the deck below. Brian waives friendly like, but Burt gives him the finger.

"Wow, Lexi is right," thinks Zander, *"that Burt is a dork."*

He watches Brian and Burt cross the deck and descend down some stairs. Zander calls the other three for a huddle to discuss the day:

Zander, "I just saw Burt and his brother, but they left to a lower deck."

Garret, "That's good. I hope we never see them again."

Lexi, "We're bound to see them; we are on this ship for five more days."

Talin, "I don't want to see Tank again. Why did he buy me that stupid drink?"

Zander, "Talin, you don't know for sure that it was from him."

Lexi, "Well, I didn't see any boys in the dining room close to Talin's age."

Garret, "Maybe it was some weird adult. You know, like we hear about on the news."

Talin, "Whether it was Tank or a weird guy, I don't like it. I'm scared." Her fingers are twirling her hair again.

"The second clue, what are we going to do about that?" asks Lexi, changing the subject.

"I don't know. Any ideas?" replies Zander. Silence. "If our parents have no idea, what can we do about it?"

After a long silence, Garret comes up with an idea. "Let's show it to our room steward. He said to call him if we have any questions."

"I don't think that's the type of question he meant," Zander says.

"Okay," Garret replies, "who's got a better idea?"

Again, silence which is broken by: "Time to go, it's late," the parents say.

When the kids go into their rooms they are shocked. The rooms have been picked up and everything is very neat and organized, definitely not the way they left them. Even the glasses are in plastic wrap again.

Lexi runs into her parents' room. "Mom, Dad, someone's been in our room. It doesn't look like it did when we left. I left the clothes I changed out of just before dinner on the floor and now they're gone. We've been robbed!"

"Lexi, it was Diego, our room steward," her mother says. "This is what the room steward does. He tidies up your room for the evening."

Talin calls out, "Look at our bed. There's an elephant on it."

Lexi hurries back into her room, not understanding why Talin is claiming there's an elephant on the bed. But there is. It's a towel folded into the shape of an elephant. Zander and Garret come into the room next after hearing the commotion, followed by their parents.

Lexi is now checking drawers for her clothes she thought were taken. She finds them. "YEAH!" She checks the bathroom. New fresh towels are hanging and everything she and Talin had left on the sink is organized in perfect rows on the shelves. "CUTE."

Garret says, "We have a rabbit on our bed and a mint."

"Mint … awesome," says Lexi.

"Mom, what animal did you get?" Talin asks.

"Ours is a swan and we got mints too."

Entering the room, Zander's dad declares, "Ours is the best, we have a hanging monkey."

And everyone goes into his room to see the hanging monkey made out of a towel.

Chapter 9 Day at Sea

DAY 2

It's morning and the kids join their parents on their respective balconies. They enjoy the view of the ocean and the warmth of the sun. Breakfast at the buffet is next and the selection is broad and good enough to satisfy whatever the kids want. They eat at a window overlooking the ocean.

"After doing your homework, what do you want to do today?" the parents ask. The kids decide to do the sports deck in the morning and the pool area in the afternoon. They have forgotten about solving the clue. The parents want to go to the spa. The fathers for a massage and the mothers for a facial treatment. Grandma wants to lie in the sun and read. So, grandpa volunteers to go with the kids.

On the sports deck, the kids play basketball, shuffle board and miniature golf. Zander uses the golf club like a hockey stick. Grandpa beats them all at ping pong. Next is the climbing wall. They excel at that.

They are finishing up at the climbing wall when Bernie appears with her parents. The kids quickly look around for her cousins, but they are nowhere to be seen.

Bernie, "Hi, Talin what are you doing?"

Talin, "I was doing the climbing wall. What are you doing?"

"I'm going to walk the track around the smoke stack with my parents. Would you like to walk with me?"

"Sure, grandpa can I walk with Bernie?"

"Where are you going?" grandpa asks.

Bernie's parents answer. "We're going to walk the track that goes around the smoke stack. It's right above us."

"Okay," grandpa says, "can I join you?"

All the grandkids join in and everybody walks the track, except the three oldest decide to run. Talin stays with Bernie.

Talin and Bernie are talking excitingly to each other. They are the same age and size and both wear black-rimmed glasses. They are both very animated and gesture a lot as they walk and talk. Talin learns Bernie lives in France.

The older kids are tired of running and join Bernie and Talin.

"Ahh…, where are your cousins?" Zander asks Bernie hesitantly, while trying to act as if he didn't care.

"They're at the swimming area. I'll join them this afternoon." replies Bernie.

Talin, seeing an opportunity to be with Bernie, says, "We're going swimming this afternoon too." Zander and Garret mutter, "Oh crud."

Bernie notices their uptightness and says, "Don't worry. If you're my friends, cousin Burt won't hurt you. He may talk tough, but he knows not to hurt my friends."

Zander and Garret aren't so sure little Bernie has that much control over Burt, but her words are reassuring. They also find out that Bernie's family is assigned to the other main dining room. So dinner won't be in the same room as Burt.

It's then lunch time. Again, there's a fine selection for the kids at the buffet. After lunch, it's change into swim suits and go to the swim area. Grandpa takes a nap near the pool. None of the Bs are around. The kids do the water slides a few times and then play in the salt water pool.

A little later Burt and Brian appear. They immediately jump into the pool. Burt starts trash talking Zander, ignoring the others. Zander sees a tattoo on Burt's shoulder and for a deflection, asks Burt about it.

Burt is more than happy to brag about his tattoo.

"I got this off base at Fort Bragg. It's a tribal lion tattoo signifying my great finesse."

"What does that mean?"

"It means I have the ability to move around people in a smooth and persuasive manner. That's how I fight."

Geez, thinks Zander, this guy is crazy. "Did your parents object?"

"They didn't know until after I got it. My dad beat me real bad."

"You mean you had a real fight with your dad?" Garret asks.

"Yeah, stupid, don't you fight with your dad?"

"Not that I can remember." replies Garret.

"Hey, have either of you ever been in a fight?"

Garret, "No, should we have been?"

"Wow. On an army base, we kids are fighting all the time. I'll take you guys on together. It should be a piece of cake."

"Why fight? What's the point of it? Plus you're much bigger than us. You should pick on people your own size," Garret persists, not sure how far he should carry on this conversation. Burt obviously doesn't handle disagreements well.

"You guys are wimps." says Burt, "I don't like weaklings or cowards. I've had a lot of fights with guys bigger than me. This will make you tougher. Besides, I haven't found anybody else around here to fight. You're it. We won't do it here; there are too many adults around. I'll let you know the time and place later." Then Burt thinks and changes his mind, "Unless I can make you two start the fight" After that comment, Burt starts moving towards Lexi and Talin at the other end of the pool.

"Lexi, Talin get out of the pool!" Zander and Garret yell.

Chapter 10 Pool Area

Lexi and Talin don't hear the boys. Burt is getting closer. He keeps looking over his shoulder at Zander and Garret and smirking. Garret hollows, **"GRANDPA, WE NEED YOU!"** Grandpa doesn't hear. Grandpa is napping.

Burt sneaks up behind Lexi and pushes her under the water. Lexi resurfaces immediately wondering who did that. She freaks when she sees it's Burt.

Burt splashes water at Talin. Talin wipes her eyes. Then she's splashed again.

"Stop that!" cries Talin. But Burt doesn't stop and says, "I'll do this for as long as it takes for your creepy cousins to come to your rescue." Burt looks back at the boys who have decided to try to do something, anything and approach Burt.

Burt turns to face the boys. "Okay wimps, what are you going to do? I'm not throwing the first punch," and he splashes Lexi and Talin again.

"Please stop." Zander pleads.

Burt does a hard splash at Zander, then Garret.

A loud high pitch girl's voice comes from the edge of the pool. "BURT, STOP BOTHERING MY FRIENDS!"

It's Bernadette with her hands on her hips looking directly at Burt with as mean a look on her face as she can do.

"Bernie, stay out of it. You can't do anything about this," says Burt."

"But I can," comes a voice approaching behind Bernie. It's her father.

He continues, "Burt, get out of the pool and go sit down. Leave these kids alone."

Surprisingly, Burt does so. Bernie's dad doesn't look like a tough guy. In fact it looks like Burt could take him in a fight, but apparently he has some ability to control Burt. Thank goodness!

Bernie gets in the pool. "Sorry about that. As long as my dad is here, Burt won't bother you."

"Why is that?" asks Zander.

"A long story," says Burt's brother Brian, who has just joined them. "All you need to know is that Bernie's dad is trustee of funds for me and Burt. Our weekly allowances come from him. I usually get mine, but Burt screws up so much, well he doesn't always get his."

Zander, "So that's the control?"

"Yes, and Burt really wants his allowance this week."

"How much is it?" asks Lexi, wanting to get in on a conversation with Brian.

"$25.00 and Burt wants it for getting another tattoo when we are in port at La Romano."

"Won't Bernie's dad object to that use of the money?" asks Lexi.

"Burt has it all planned out. He found online a tattoo place close to the port. He's going to sneak away and put it on his butt, so his parents and uncle won't know."

"But you know," Zander says.

"Sure, but I'm not telling, just like I won't help you guys in a fight with Burt. I've been beaten and kicked so many times; I just go along with him and try not to upset him."

"Enough about Burt," says Bernie, "Let's have fun."

The four grandkids, Brian and Bernie swim and go down the water slide all afternoon. Then it is dinner time and the four grandkids get to have a table by themselves. Talin looks around for Tank. She doesn't see him.

The menu is again unusual for the kids. They select shrimp for the appetizer. Their reactions to the main course selections include: tilapia ("yuck, fish"), shrimp ("we had that for appetizer"), chicken a la grecque ("maybe"), linguini with Italian sausage, ("no way"), grilled tofu steak, ("altered soybeans, not for us") and beef brisket in gravy ("are you serious"). They all have the chicken with French fries on the side.

They think dessert, however, is great. They order vanilla crème brulee which was baked vanilla ice cream garnished with assorted berries.

Right before dessert, Talin is served a drink. It's delivered by the same Pilipino waiter as the night before. 'Don' is on his nametag. He says, "For you, madam, from a secret admirer. It's called 'banana bonkers'. It has grapefruit juice, lemon sherbet, ice and of course, bananas."

"Who is this from?" Talin demands.

The waiter replies, "Sorry, I'm not allowed to say. Enjoy." The waiter leaves.

Talin stands on her chair and looks around the room. She doesn't see Tank anywhere.

"Sit down," the others tell Talin. "You'll cause us to lose our separate table privileges."

Talin sits, tastes the drink and declares, "It's wonderful." She lets the others try it. They like it, too.

Chapter 11 Magic Show

After dinner there's a magic show in the ship's theater. The magician turns a whole bunch of green colored plants into different colors. Zander says to Garret, who is again dressed in green, "Wish you could do that."

Garret ignores him. He is thinking about the clue. *What could it mean?*

There's a floating/levitation illusion. Garret says, "Just like Lexi in gymnastics, but Lexi can do it faster." They all laugh.

The women assistant is sawed in half. "There are really two girls," Zander remarks.

A volunteer from the audience is placed in a guillotine. His head does not come off when the blade is lowered. But the carrot next to his head is cut in half.

The magician then performs a mind reading trick. An audience member randomly selects a card and shows it to the audience and magician's assistant. Everyone in the theater knows the card, except the magician. The assistant sits in a chair and the magician says he is going to read her mind. He stands behind her and puts his fingers on her head, on each side of her temple area. After awhile he declares the identity of the card and he is correct. Applause.

"How does he do that?" the kids ask grandpa.

Grandpa replies, "It's Morse code. She clenches her jaw quickly and it means a dot. A longer clinch is a dash.

The magician can feel her jaw clinching by touching the temple area of her head. Try it."

The kids try it. It works.

"But how does that tell him what the card is?" Garret asks.

"As I said," grandpa replies, "It's Morse code. Each combination of a quick clinch or longer clinch means a dot or dash used for Morse code. The different combinations of quick or long clinches are in place of the dots and dashes used for the different letters of the alphabet."

On stage, the magician is restoring a newspaper he had just torn to pieces. Garret says, "I know how that is done."

Garret is thinking: *dots and lines can be a code for letters of the alphabet. It's called Morse code. Hmmmmm*

The magician finishes the show with Houdini's famous metamorphoses trick. He is hand-cuffed and placed in a bag which is tied at the top. Then he's lowered into a trunk which is then padlocked by volunteers from the audience. To add to the effect, the audience volunteers examine and vouch that the padlocks are real.

His assistant stands on top on the trunk with a sheet. She counts, "1", raises the sheet over her head, counts "2" and then on "3" the sheet is lowered and the magician is standing on top of the trunk. He then unlocks the padlocks, opens the trunk, unties the bag and his assistant appears! Applause!

The grandkids appear impressed until grandpa tells them the locks are real, but the trunk has a secret door on the back, the bag has no bottom and the hand cuffs are fake.

"Grandpa, you're a spoiler," says Talin, "but thanks anyway."

"That's okay Talin. Magic is more about presentation than the actual trick. The trick always has a secret to it. There's no such thing as real magic. It's the way the trick is presented that fools you. Are you having a good time?"

They leave the show and Garret is excited.

"We've got to find a Morse code," he tells the others.

"Who's Morse code?" asks Talin. "Is he my secret admirer?"

"It's not a person," replies Garret, "It's a series of dots and lines that indicate letters."

Lexi catches on, "You mean the second clue could be solved by a Morse code, whatever that is?"

"Yes," Garret replies. "I need to Google Morse code."

"Hopefully, we'll have internet when we get into port tomorrow morning," Zander says.

The rest of the evening is spent with the parents in the Atrium Lounge listening to the Motown Band. The kids are now free to roam without an adult now. But with Burt on the ship, Zander and Garret were okay staying with the parents. Likewise, Talin wanted to avoid running into Tank. Lexi actually liked the Motown music, which is popular music by African-American artists from the 1960s and 70s.

Chapter 12 Cayman Island

DAY 3

The next morning the ship is already anchored near Cayman Island when Garret wakes up. He goes to his parent's balcony and sees that the ship is not next to a pier, but anchored offshore. Strange, but Garret is more interested in finding out about the Morse code. Back to his room, he checks his Ipad. There's internet service! He googles 'Morse code' and finds that it is a code used in the 1800s until the 1930s for sending messages by dots and dashes. That was before radios and was mostly used by the telegraph system. It was also before actual letters and numbers could be transmitted.

He compares the dots and lines on the bookmark clue with a Morse code chart. He writes a letter beside each line.

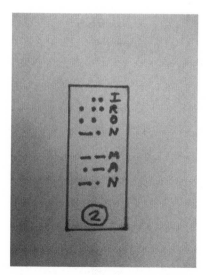

Iron Man, what does that mean? Thinks Garret.

At breakfast, a table for everybody next to a window is available. The kids see the town of George Town a short distance from the ship. The ship is not moving.

"Why aren't we at a dock?" Zander asks.

Grandpa answers, "There isn't a dock big enough for our ship in the Cayman Islands. We are at anchor."

"How do we get ashore then?" asks Lexi.

"The ship's life boats are used as tenders to take us from the ship to one of three tender ports in George Town. It's a 15 minute ride."

"Great, we will get to ride in a life boat," Talin adds excitedly, "What will we do here?"

"We can't do much because the ship is here for only six hours," says grandma, while looking over a Cayman Island excursion brochure. She continues, "We've booked the Stingray City tour and I'd like to look in the duty free shops in George Town."

"That sounds good," the other mothers agree.

"What's Stingray City?" asks Garret.

"It's a place in the ocean near here with shallow sandbars where you can swim with and feed stingrays. Grandpa and I did it on a previous cruise. I know you'll like it." Grandma answers.

"Can't stingrays sting?" Talin asks, "Isn't that why they're called stingrays?"

Grandpa answers this time. "These stingrays are used to tourists who feed them. Just don't step on one or touch its tail. The tail is where the stinging barbs are."

"Not sure I'm going to like this," says Talin.

"You'll be fine," grandma assures her, "If I can do it, you can too."

"Finish up here," says grandpa, "We'll leave the ship shortly. You'll have to do your homework when we return."

While the parents discuss the shops in George Town they want to explore, the kids discuss the clue; 'Iron Man' that Garret has come up with.

"I think we're at a dead end," says Zander.

"Yes," Lexi agrees, "unless… we can figure out who planted the clues."

"The first clue was left under our door. Grandpa was with us, so it isn't him. Could it have been grandma or one of our parents?" asks Garret.

"They've never done a scavenger hunt for us," Zander responds.

"Grandpa likes scavenger hunts. He could have given the clue to one of our parents to put under the door while we were with him on the ship tour," says Lexi.

Garret considers this, and then says, "I don't think so. He didn't recognize the Morse code clue and I believe him. If it was grandpa's scavenger hunt, he would have given us a hint when he saw we were stumped. He couldn't have known the Morse code would be used in the magic show."

"Then we're at a dead end," Zander says again.

Chapter 13 Stingray City

The kids enjoy the up and down ride over the waves in the lifeboat used as a tender boat. Shortly after that trip, it's a ride in a bigger two level boat with an open top deck out to a sandbar in the middle of the sea. They feel the power of the sea as it moves the boat up, down and sideways.

"On the ship you hardly feel any movement at all," observes Garret. It's not lost on the kids that it's a beautiful sunny 80 degree day with the sea looking a turquoise color. When the boat arrives at the sand bar, there are many other similar boats that have taken cruise passengers to Stingray City. They are parked in a circle around a large sand bar. The water is crystal clear and you can see the bottom of the sea all around. In the middle are people in waist deep water with hundreds of stingrays swimming around them. Our boat slowly pushes onto the edge of the sandbar and stops. A gangplank is lowered and passengers start down it into the waist deep water, some having been given food to feed the stingrays.

On the top deck, Talin notices what looks like a shark in the distance on the other side of the boat. Pointing to it, she asks, "Grandpa, is that a shark?"

"Not sure, I'll find out," grandpa replies.

Grandpa gets the attention of one of the excursion crew members and points to the large fish in the deeper water.

"Yes," he replies, "that is a shark, but he won't bother, the sand bar is much too shallow for him."

That's enough to discourage Talin; she's not going into the water. No way. So grandpa stays on board with her while the others feed and touch the stingrays.

Late morning, it's back to George Town where everyone hurries, according to the women, through the duty free shops.

"What's duty free mean?" asks Garret.

"It means there's no taxes on merchandize to travelers," grandpa answers. "The goods are therefore cheaper and as long as you don't buy too much, there's no import tax to bring the items back into the United States. It's a way to encourage trade and competition among world markets."

"I don't understand the last part."

"Sorry, don't understand it myself. It's just that the merchandise is cheaper because there are no taxes on it."

Garret is proud of himself. He came up with a question grandpa couldn't answer.

We tender back to the ship. To get onboard, each passenger has to show their Ship and Sail card. The card has a picture of the passenger on it. It goes smoothly until it's Talin's turn. Her picture hardly looks like her. After a few questions of her parents, security lets her board.

After doing school work under grandma's supervision and changing into clothes for the evening, the kids and grandma go to the Atrium lounge. Grandpa and their fathers are already there, reserving a table next to the stage. The adults get cocktails and the kids get sodas.

On stage three women are playing violins. Grandpa loves it, but the others aren't so sure. Grandma hates violins. The kids don't like it either. They don't recognize any of the music. It's classical. Bernie and her parents appear. Grandpa invites them to the table and introduces everyone.

Immediately, Bernie talks about the submarine tour her family did today.

"It was awesome. What did you do?'Bernie asks, looking at Talin.

"We went to Stingray City," which Talin describes but leaves out the part that she didn't go into the water.

Bernie realizing there aren't enough seats and not impressed by the violins, says to the kids "Let's go somewhere else?"

Lexi says, "Yes, anywhere but here. Can we, mom?"

Her mother replies, "Okay, but you all have to stay together."

Before Bernie and the kids leave, Zander, a little uncomfortable being away from the adults, asks, "Where are your cousins, Burt and Brian?"

"They're at the exercise room with their mother. She works out a lot and Burt does too."

Cool, thinks Zander; the coast is clear. *We'll just stay away from the exercise room.*

Bernie, "Let's go to the game center." And she starts leading the way.

"Wait, we don't have any money," Lexi says.

Bernie stops, turns and rolling her eyes, says "You don't need money. Just use your Ship and Sail card."

"Yeah, sure," Lexi replies and without saying anything, she runs back to her parents.

Permission is given for each of the grandkids to spend up to $5.00 on their Ship and Sail cards.

Chapter 14 Game Room

At the game room, the kids take turns playing various machines. Most plays cost a dollar. While one plays, the others watch. This way the money lasts longer.

Against one wall is a line of pin ball machines. Lexi wants to play one.

"Which one should I play?" she asks.

The five kids walk along the row of machines examining each one. Zander recites the names of each. "Monster Bash, Terminator 2, Space Ship, Iron Man, the Wizard, …"

"STOP!" yells Garret, "Did you say 'Iron Man'?"

"Yeah," Zander replies, "Iron Man; it's right there." Zander points to the machine. "Do you think it has anything to do with the Morse code clue?"

"I don't know," says Garret, "but what else on this ship could mean Iron Man?"

After filling Bernie in about the clue, they examine the machine. "Maybe you have to play it to get the next clue," Lexi suggests and inserts her Ship and Sail card for one play. Everyone watches Lexi play the Iron Man pinball machine. After she finishes, nobody has come up with any idea about the clue.

They examine the outside of the machine. Nothing. The machine is a floor model raised only about two inches above the floor. "Talin, you're the smallest. Look underneath," Zander asks.

Talin gives Zander a mean look. She doesn't like being called little again, but lies on the floor to look underneath.

"It's dark, I can't see anything."

"Then feel with your hands."

This is not something Talin cares to do. *What if there's a bug underneath!* But the others are counting on her and she doesn't want to show fear in front of Bernie. If she doesn't do it, then Bernie will be asked and if Bernie does it, then, Talin thinks, *I'll be the one disappointing everybody.*

Talin nervously extends her hand slowly under the machine and right away feels a piece of paper on the bottom. *Great, I did it!* She gives paper to Garret.

"Way to go, Talin," says Zander.

"No problem, no problem at all," replies Talin with look of success on her face.

Garret looks at the paper and announces. "It has the number 3 in a circle on it. It's the third clue!"

Everybody watches Garret unfold the paper.

"What does it say?"

"It doesn't say anything; I think it's another code."

After everyone studies it for awhile, Bernie has an idea. "The most commonly used letter is 'E'. she says, "I know this from watching 'Wheel of Fortune'. So replace the symbol used the most often with 'E' Also try 'T' and 'A' the other most commonly used letters. Maybe that will get you closer to the answer."

Everybody tries Bernie's suggestion. Nothing comes close to making any sense. Disappointed, they go to the Atrium Bar to meet with their parents.

The route they go takes them by the computer bar, karaoke room and casino.

It's crowded and then approaching them they see B&B, Burt and Brian! B&B spot them and approach. Burt's right arm hangs naturally along his side, but his hand is in a clinched fist! The boys see this but with so many people around, Burt wouldn't start a fight here, right?

Chapter 15 Captain's Table

Burt raises his clenched fist in front of Zander's face and says, "See this? This fist is going to be in your face! Go for the first punch, wimp."

Okay, Zander thinks, *if he's not going to throw the first punch, what have I got to be afraid of.*

Zander stands up straight, looks Burt into his eyes and says, "I'm a man of my word. Are you?"

"Yeah, what of it?" Burt replies.

"You say you're not going to throw the first punch?" Zander asks assertively.

"That's right," Burt replies, "You've got to start it. That way I'm justified in beating the crap out of you. I figure I can duck out of the way of your first swing and if I don't, you don't have enough power to hurt me much anyway....wimp."

Zander remains ramrod straight keeping his eyes focused on Burt eyes, says loudly, "Burt, I don't want to fight you. You'd beat me easily anyway and what would we gain from it? I'm not throwing any punch. I'd rather we'd be friends and do things together. How about it?"

Garret, Lexi, Talin, Bernie and Brian stand silently and are nervous about what might happen next.

Burt breaks eye contact with Zander, looks down and says softly, "I'll think about it." Burt is not used to this type of response. The person he is threatening wants to be friends. How can that be? Burt walks on. Brian smiles at Lexi and follows Burt.

Garret breaks the group's silence and says, "Way to go, Zander. You made him promise not to throw the first punch and you stood up to him."

This makes Zander feel better. *I'll try to make him a friend.*

As the kids continue to the Atrium Lounge to meet with their parents, Talin asks Bernie about seeing her again after dinner.

"Sorry, Talin," Bernie replies, "I have to go to a family dinner in the specialty restaurant. Today is my grandparents' 50th wedding anniversary."

"Will Burt be there, too?" Zander asks.

"Yes," replies Bernie. Zander is relieved.

"What's a specialty restaurant?" asks Talin.

"It's a French restaurant on deck 9. It's very fancy and you have to pay extra to eat there. It's not included in the cruise price. You also need reservations in advance. I'm excited about it because I live in France and like French food. My mother makes it all the time. Does your family have reservations to eat there? "

"I don't think so," replies Zander who's thinking, *besides, grandma would never let grandpa spend money on something like that.*

When the kids get to the Atrium lounge, the three violinists are playing a modern song that Talin and Bernie both know. They try to sing along, but they don't like this rendition.

Bernie leaves with her parents. Talin's family gets in line for the dining room. It's the same table arrangement as the night before. Kids at one table and the adults at another. The kids notice a bearded gentleman in a white uniform sitting with others at the large round table in the middle of the dining hall. He appears to have the attention of the others at his table.

"Who's that?" Lexi asks.

"That's the ship captain," grandpa replies, "The ship captain sometimes eats with the passengers. You may also see him walking around the ship. It adds to the cruising experience. How do you like the cruise so far?"

Lexi thinks, *Well, there's Burt the bully, the giant that torments Talin and the obnoxious room steward, but then there's Brian,* "Great," she responds.

At the table, Talin gets another drink from the Pilipino waiter who says it is a PB Banana smoothie. It's made with peanut butter, banana and oatmeal. "Yuk," Talin says after tasting it. This time the main course is wild game. The three older grandkids decide to experiment and share, ordering roast duck, quail and ostrich. Talin stays with the chicken.

The dining room has square pillars with mirrors on all sides. As Garret is looking at himself in a mirror, he suddenly has an idea. "Zander, give me the third clue." Zander gives it to him. Garret holds it up to the mirror. "I solved the clue," he says excitedly, "Look!"

Chapter 16 Exercise Room

Everyone looks and they see in the mirror the reverse image of third clue.

ROWINGFOREXERCISE

"I don't get it," says Talin.

"It says 'rowing for exercise', Garret explains, "We need to go to the exercise room and find a rowing machine."

"You're right," says Lexi, "Garret, you solved the third clue."

Talin is depressed. She wants to solve a clue.

Garret goes to the adults' table and asks if anyone would take the kids to the exercise room after dinner. "Why?" the parents ask. "Because kids can't enter without an adult." Garret explains.

"I understand that," his dad says, "but why the exercise room?"

Garret tells them about the scavenger hunt and the mirror clue.

"Maybe later," his father replies, "after dinner we're going to the evening show in the theater and we want to arrive early to get seats up front. A metal band is performing that was one of our favorites when we were younger."

"Then afterwards?" Garret pleads.

"We'll see," his dad says.

Grandpa speaks, "I'll take you after dinner Garret. I won't mind missing tonight's show. If you kids don't care for the show tonight, we can do something else. I want you to have a good time on this trip."

Geez, will grandpa lay off the have a good time stuff, Garret thinks, but says, "Thank you, Grandpa."

After dinner, the grandkids and grandpa take off for the exercise room. Grandma, who doesn't think she will like the show, decides to join them. The parents head for the theater. Knowing that Burt is at a family dinner party, the kids aren't worried about running into him. It's good grandma decided to go because Lexi and Talin otherwise wouldn't have gotten in. You have to go through a men's or ladies' locker room to get to the exercise area and no kid is admitted without an adult with them.

The exercise room has two rows of treadmills and bikes facing a glass wall overlooking the front of the boat. All you see is ocean. Behind these are weight machines, step masters, and two glass-walled rooms each with one wall of mirrors. One room is used for exercise classes and the other for weight lifting.

It's evening, so there are only a couple of other people using the exercise room and darn, one is on the only rowing machine in the room. While waiting for the rowing machine to become available, the kids race on the treadmills and have a weight lifting contest.

"Zander, you better beef up for your fight with Burt," Garret teases him.

"Not funny, Garret," Zander replies.

The rowing machine becomes available and the kids run to it. Yes, underneath the seat as expected, there's a clue. Talin insists on being the one to retrieve it. She pulls it out and opens it. She studies it but doesn't say anything.

"What does it say?" the others plead.

Talin, still looking at the clue, is mouthing something, but saying nothing.

Lexi growing impatient rips the note out of Talin's hand and studies it. "This is too hard," she says and throws it up in the air. Zander and Garret retrieve the note and are also stumped.

Chapter 17 Tank Rescue

Written on clue number 4 is:

Le chat dans la chapeau par Docteur Seuss dans la art gallerie d'art

"Is it another code?" asks Talin.

"No, I think it's a foreign language," suggests Garret.

"It's probably Spanish because we're going to the Dominican Republic," Lexi mentions. "Who do we know who speaks Spanish?"

"Our room steward!" says Garret.

"Lexi, you ask him," suggests Zander, "You're on good terms with him."

"Yeah, right," answers Lexi, "we all go together."

"Okay," says Zander, "Grandpa and grandma, we're ready to go and we need to stop at our rooms. Hey, where are they?"

The kids look around and see grandma on the treadmill and grandpa's lifting weights.

"Okay," the grandparents reply and everybody leaves the exercise room.

The grandparents go to catch the end of the metal band show. The kids are given permission to go around on their own, provided they stay together. The grandparents don't know that's exactly what the grandkids want to do, stay together.

The kids go to their rooms and find Diego in Lexi's room bent over a bed carefully folding a towel into some kind of animal. Lexi busts into the room and says excitedly, "Diego."

Diego jumps almost to the ceiling having been so occupied making his creation and cries, "You scared me."

"Sorry," says Lexi, "but can you translate this Spanish for us?" and shows him the clue.

Diego looks at clue number 4 and snarls, "You kids from the United States are so unworldly you don't know difference between languages! This isn't Spanish, it's French. Use your brains."

Suffering from the put down, Lexi again says "Sorry," *thinking how many times do I have to say sorry to him,* "we didn't know. Can you translate it anyway?"

"No, I can't." Diego responds angrily and unravels his partially made towel creature, "I shall make you a stupid animal. Yes, a turkey, the dumbest animal on the planet."

"Let's get out of here," Lexi says and they leave wondering what to do for a French translation of the clue.

"I know," says Talin, "I bet Bernie or her parents know French. They said they were from France."

"Good idea, Talin," says Garret, "We'll ask them, but they're at their family dinner tonight. We'll have to wait until we see them tomorrow."

Talin is glowing. She may not have solved the clue, but she came up with a way to get the answer.

Part of deck 10 is without a roof and when the kids walk through a door to the outside they hear a faint call of 'help me'.

"Somebody needs help," says Zander. "It's coming from up above us."

They run up the stairs to a sun deck where it's dark and nobody is around. Again they hear, "Help me," but this time it's louder.

"It's coming from the stern on the other side of that wall," Zander points.

They go around the corner and there's Tank. He's flat on his back and there's a crushed chair underneath him.

"What happened?" Zander asks.

"I lost my head phones, so I sit out here where there's nobody around and the sound from my video games won't bother others. I was gaming while enjoying this beautiful night, looking at the stars and listening to the ocean when this deck chair broke. I guess it wasn't sturdy enough for me. Anyway, the sides of the chair are narrower than my waist and are pinned against me. It makes it impossible for me to turn to the side so I can get up. This is so embarrassing. Oh, it's you Talin. How are you?"

"So how can we help you?" asks Zander, "Do you want us to go for help?"

"No, no, don't go for help, at least not yet. If the cruise ship people find out about this, they might ban me from future cruises. They say I'm too big for the cruise ship facilities, but since I was already booked, it was too late for them to refuse me. This happened at check-in at the cruise terminal. I don't want to give them any reason to black list me for future cruises."

"So what do you want us to do?" asks Zander.

"Maybe with your help, we can break the side arm of this chair. Then I can roll to my side and get up."

Zander, Garret, Lexi and Talin each grab a part of the chair arm. Not much seems to happen until Tank adds his strength to the task and then .... 'Crack', the arm breaks off from the chair. Tank rolls to his side and struggles to get up. The kids, except Talin, help him stand up, feeling nothing but fat as they push against his side. Tank pretends that they are really helping, but Zander thinks he could have gotten up on his own.

"Thank you very much," says Tank, "and I will thank you even more if you don't report this to anyone connected with the ship."

"We won't," Zander replies, "Do you need help getting down the steps?"

"No I can make it, but slowly. You kids go ahead and thank you."

Chapter 18 TEEN CLUB

The kids leave Tank and return to the lower deck. Zander says, "Talin, he's really a nice guy. I don't know why you don't like him."

"He's gross." Talin replies.

They stand along the deck railing and for awhile feel the cool breeze, listen to the quiet roar of the ocean and enjoy the night sky with the moon and more stars than they've ever seen before.

"Why are there so many stars?" Lexi asks, "At home, there aren't as many."

"At home the lights of the city partially light up the sky and prevent you from seeing the dimmer stars." Garret replies, "There's always the same number of stars, but the darker the sky is, the more you can see."

They stand quietly just looking and listening until,

"Okay, that's enough," says Talin, "Let's do something."

Lexi has an idea, "Let's go to the teen club. Burt is at his family party, so we don't have to worry about running into him."

They go down to the teen club and there's nobody there except the DJ and a bartender for the teen bar. Even though Zander is the only teenager, there's no objection for all of them entering.

"Hi, kids. Come on in," says the DJ who looks Asian but talks in perfect English, "What music would you like to hear?" He's glad to have customers.

Talin quickly answers with the name of her favorite current song.

"Got it. I'll play it," and he scrolls down on his Ipad.

Zander decides to play big shot. He jumps onto a bar stool, slaps his Ship and Sail card down on the bar and says to the bartender, "Four beers, please," The bartender, another Asian, says, "No way mister. Only non alcoholic drinks are served here."

Zander smiles, liking that he was called mister and says, "I know that. I just wanted to say it. Make it four banana bonkers instead."

"Zander, those drinks are expensive. Should you be doing this?" says Garret as he and the others also get on bar stools.

"Grandpa wants us to have a good time. So let's have a good time."

Just then, Talin's song starts and Talin sings along in perfect harmony. After the song is over, the bartender, while serving the drinks, says to Talin, "You should enter the karaoke contest. It's right next door."

"What's the prize?" Garret asks.

"I'm not sure; sometimes it's a free drink at any bar on the ship."

Another song comes on and Lexi, instead of dancing, does round offs on the dance floor. Garret tries some acrobatics too, but it's funny when he tries and the others laugh.

Lexi and Garret return to the bar and over the loud music, the kids do some toasting and talk about the cruise. They are disappointed there aren't more kids their ages on the cruise. Especially someone else for Burt to pick on. They make jokes about Tank, the room steward and the 3 Bs.

Talin wants to go to the karaoke club. At the karaoke club they learn they can't get in without an adult because alcohol is served. Bummer. "What should we do now?" Talin asks and then suggests going back into the teen club where she could sing along again.

"Lame," Lexi says, "there's nobody in there. We might as well go meet our parents. The show should be over by now."

The show is over and everybody admits they are tired and ready to retire to their rooms. However, grandpa, who had a nap today, suggests going to the piano bar. He has no takers.

Upon returning to their rooms, Lexi fails to notice the French/English translation book on the desk. Instead she sees the towel shaped into a turkey on her bed. 'Insulting' she mummers and throws it on the floor.

Talin, however, notices the book and shows it to Lexi. Lexi takes it and immediately goes to her cousins room with Talin following and shows it to the boys.

"Where'd you get that?" asks Zander.

"I gave it to her," says Talin.

"Okay, where did you get it?"

"It was on our desk." Talin replies. "Strange things are happening on this ship."

"That's for sure," adds Garret.

Garret has a plan and gets the French clue out. "Lexi, I'll spell each word one by one and you look up what it means in English. Zander, you write down the words that Lexi finds. Talin, you stand at the door and listen for grandma or a parent coming."

This goes on until they finish all the words in the clue.

"Read it Zander," Talin says with excitement. Zander reads:

THE CAT IN THE HAT BY DOCTOR SEUSS IN THE ART GALLERY

Talin, "What the heck does that mean?"

Lexi, "Is there an art gallery on this ship?"

Garret, "The clue refers to a book, not a painting."

Zander, "Why was the clue written in French? It's hard enough in English."

Lexi, "Why did this book appear in my room? Who knew we needed it?"

Lexi's mom appears in the room and asks what is going on. The kids respond 'nothing'. Lexi asks her, "Mom, is there an art gallery on the ship?"

"Yes, I believe so. If there is one, it would be near the gift shops on the Lido deck. The same level as the Atrium Lounge. Why do you ask?"

"No reason, just wondering," says Lexi and she and Talin go back to their room.

Chapter 19 Amber Cove

DAY 4

On the morning of day 4 of the cruise, the ship is approaching Amber Cove which is on the North side of the Dominican Republic. It's another beautiful day and the kids watch the shoreline coming closer from their parents' balconies. The shoreline is a continuous band of white sand with pale green trees and smaller vegetation maybe a hundred feet inland. The ship is moving slowly but finally a large pier comes into view. Fortunately, our balconies are on the side of the ship that will be next to the pier. Grandpa hollers from his balcony, "CAN YOU HEAR ME? I WANT TO EXPLAIN THE DOCKING PROCEDURE."

Zander's dad responds, "Yes, we can hear you and so can everybody else on the ship. We can see that we are docking."

In a lower voice, grandpa continues, "I know you are watching but I want to explain what you are seeing."

He continues without needing to be asked, "The port side which we are on also means the side of a ship that usually parks next to a port. There is no need for tug boats to push the ship to the dock. This is because the cruise ship has side thrusters below the water line on each side of the bow and stern which are propulsion systems that move the ship sideways."

"I didn't know that," says Lexi, which is all grandpa needs to continue.

"It's a slow process because if the ship as big and heavy as ours were to bump into the pier, the pier would have no chance."

When the ship is finally next to the dock, ropes are being tossed to men on the pier. Grandpa continues, "The small ropes are called heaving lines and have monkey fists or pouches of sand on the ends. They are tossed from the ship to dockhands on the pier. The dockhands use the heaving lines to pull larger ropes called hawsers or mooring lines onto the dock."

The mooring lines are the thickest ropes the kids have ever seen. They see the dockhands struggle with the huge ropes which have lopes at the ends and place them over bumpers on the dock. Eight mooring lines are used to tie the ship to the dock.

As the mooring lines become tight, grandpa explains, "The crew on the boat is using electric wrenches to pull the mooring lines tight. Pretty neat, huh?"

Next, two gangplanks are pulled out from the side of the ship below us and we are docked.

"Let's go to breakfast," Grandpa finally says.

After breakfast and an hour of grandma working with the grandkids' homework; everyone leaves the ship and goes ashore to Amber Cove. Lexi leaves the French translation book on the desk with a note that says, 'Thank you' and draws a smiley face.

As passengers leave the ship there is a photographer taking pictures of each group with the ship in the background. The four grandkids get a picture of themselves together.

Amber Cove is a tourist stop for cruise ships with multiple pools, water slides, bars, lounges, shops and cabanas. The facilities and harbor on it were built at a cost of <u>85 million dollars</u>.

There's no sign of any of the Bs and the grandkids first use the zip line which goes over the pools. Next are the water slides and then a break for lunch during which grandpa informs everyone that the town next to Amber Cove, called Puerto Plata is the first European settlement in the Americas. In addition, it is where Christopher Columbus is believed to have first landed in 1492. The grandkids hardly care but like the fact that they are in an area of great historical significance.

After lunch it's back to the largest pool. The parents sun themselves and the grandkids take to the water. When Zander takes a break and is drying himself off, he notices Talin playing with Bernie in the pool. He looks around and sees Burt, Brian and their family directly across on the other side of the pool. At the same time, Burt sees Zander and immediately motions with his head for Zander to go in a certain direction. Zander ignores him and says to his parents, "I'm tired of this place. Can we go somewhere else?"

Just then Talin runs up to her parents with Bernie behind her and asks, "Can we go to the Dolphin encounter? Bernie went there this morning and it sounds cool."

"Yes," Bernie adds excitedly, "I got to pet and kiss a dolphin!"

Now Lexi appears and hearing Bernie, says, "I'll probably never get a chance to swim with a dolphin again, ever. Can we go there?"

Before the parents can respond, Zander takes advantage of the situation and adds that he wants to do it too.

Grandma's reaction is that it's probably expensive, but grandpa reminds her that we want the kids to have a good time. When the kids' parents say they will pay for this excursion; it's all settled. We're going to the dolphin encounter.

Except for grandpa, who announces that he'll stay behind because there's a hammock in the shade over there (and he points) that he considers a wonderful place to take a nap.

At a place called Ocean World, which is a short shuttle ride from Amber Cove, the grandkids indeed get to swim with the dolphins in a waist deep pool. Their parents and grandma enjoy it too. There are two dolphins, both of which seem to ignore Talin, but finally with the help of an instructor she gets to kiss one.

They also take in exhibits featuring sea lions and sharks. Then a big surprise; the place has aquatic balls! Each grandkid gets inside a rubber ball bigger than they are and walk on the water while inside the ball.

By the time everybody gets back to the pool, they find grandpa still in the hammock, but awake and with a pink colored drink in his hand that has a little umbrella in it. Talin wants and gets the umbrella. Zander looks around for Burt, but it appears they and most other passengers have returned to the ship.

This time Talin has no trouble boarding. The security officer remembers her and her parents from the day before.

Chapter 20 Art Gallery

After everyone has showered and changed clothes, it is time to go to dinner.

Again the kids get their own table and again a waiter not theirs and with a 'Don' nametag brings <u>all</u> the kids a drink. It's red in color and Don explains it's a Red Delight. "It has strawberry puree, lemon juice and" lowering his voice says quietly, "an energy drink in it." The kids like the energy drink part and fortunately for them; their parents, who are at a table a distance away, don't hear.

"Who's it from?" Lexi asks, thinking she knows.

"Don gives the same reply as before, "I'm not allowed to tell you. Enjoy."

The kids look around but they don't see Tank. They do enjoy the drink, especially Talin who acts with a lot of enthusiasm during dinner. The dinner menu again lists some unusual selections the kids have never heard of, but one selection is a steak dish, which they all order.

After dinner, according to the plan they hatched out, the kids ask their parents if they can go to the art gallery. Grandpa who is planning on buying everybody an after dinner drink in the Atrium Bar where the violins are performing again, says, "Sounds good, I'm glad the kids are into looking at professional paintings. Come to the Atrium Bar when you're done."

They locate it where Lexi's mom said it might be. There are many paintings on the walls and in stacks, none of which interest them or are of Seuss's Cat in the Hat.

"What do we do now?" asks Garret.

"Let's ask the lady at the counter," suggests Talin.

"That could be embarrassing, I don't want to do it," says Lexi.

"Likewise," both Zander and Garret state.

"All right," Talin says because she wants to be responsible for solving one of the clues. Talin walks up to the counter and boldly asks the lady if she has a painting of The Cat in the Hat. Talin displays her best 'please help me' look.

"Cat in the Hat!" the lady exclaims and she is all excited, "Just a minute," and she starts typing on her computer. "Nobody has ever gotten this far. Unbelievable!"

The kids are amazed. Something has been triggered. Why is the lady so excited? Talin shrugs her shoulders at the others. They shrug their shoulders back.

The counter lady prints something out and hands it to Talin. It's another clue.

On the printout is the following:

QJDUVSF PG UIF DSVJTF TIJQ

XJUI DPEF J MPWF ZPV JT GSFF

"What the heck does this mean?" says Garret.

"These clues are getting harder and stupider," says Lexi.

Before leaving the Art Gallery, Garret asks the counter lady what the paper she gave them means. The lady smiles back and says, "I did my job; the rest is up to you."

"What is up to us?" Garret persists.

"Sorry," she replies, "I'm not allowed to say, but if you've gotten this far, I'm sure you can do the rest." The kids tell their parents they'll be at a table in the hallway. No they don't need anything.

The four of them study the new clue at the table. "Let's try what Bernie said," says Talin, "the most common letters are e, t and a."

Garret, "Lexi, first draw underlines for each group of letters. Then I'll tell you how many of each letter there is."

Lexi does as Garret says and then they substitute e, t and a for the most popular letters. They get this:

_T_ _ _ _ _E A_ _ _E _ _T _E_ _ _ _A

_T_ _ A_ _E T _A_E _A_ T_ _ _EE

It doesn't work and the kids are frustrated. Just then grandpa walks by on his way to a bathroom. "Grandpa, we need help," says Garret.

"What is it?"

Garret explains the latest clue they found in the scavenger hunt and that they are stomped. Grandpa looks it over, sits down and asks for a pencil. After a few notations on the paper, he says, "I've got it. The most common three letter word is 'the' and the most common letter is E. Using these guidelines, you have one three letter word ending with the most used letter E. The word is 'the' which gives you the rest of the ts and hs in the cipher."

"Cipher? What's a cipher?" asks Lexi.

"It's a code for something in writing. Each letter in the code stands for another letter in the alphabet. This one that you have is rather simple."

Simple, the kids think, *we are insulted*!

Grandpa explains, "For the 3 letters U, I, F, if you guess they stand for 'the' it shows you that each letter in the code is the letter 'after' the real letter it stands for. When you apply that rule you see the two letter before 'the' is 'of' and the rest of the cipher starts to make sense. Here let me finish it for you, this is fun."

Lexi snatches the paper away from grandpa, "No, let us finish it. It's our scavenger hunt."

Oh oh, the other kids wonder if Lexi just made a mistake.

"No problem," says grandpa, "let me know if I can be of any further help."

Grandpa leaves for the bathroom and the kids breathe in relief.

Applying grandpa's suggestion the following solution to the cipher is revealed:

PICTURE OF THE CRUISE SHIP

WITH CODE I LOVE YOU IS FREE

"Big help this is!" exclaims Lexi in frustration, "we solve the clue only to find another puzzle!"

"Quiet, Lexi," Garret thinks, "has anyone noticed a cruise ship picture anywhere on the boat?"

"There's some paintings of old sail boats in some of the art work on the walls of the stairways," says Zander.

"And there were some paintings of boats in the art gallery," adds Talin.

"Yeah, but the clue says 'picture of the cruise ship' so I don't think paintings of old sail boats would apply," says Garret.

Zander has a thought, "The prior clue said Art Gallery. This one says picture, not a painting. Picture is a photograph and the only place I can think of with pictures around here is the photo gallery right next to the Art Gallery."

Just then, Grandpa returns and asks if they solved the cipher.

"Yes we did, grandpa," says Garret, "and we need to go to the photo gallery. Will you let our parents know? We'll be right back."

"What about coming into the piano bar, there's room and the piano player will play whatever song you want."

"No thank you." says Garret, "We're on a mission."

"Okay, but all of you stay together," grandpa replies.

Chapter 21 Casino

Back to the other end of the boat the kids find the photo shop. It's a place where ship photographers display pictures they have been taking of the passengers during the cruise. All are for sale of course and there are hundreds.

"Why would anyone buy a picture when you can take pictures on your phone?" Lexi wonders. "Our parents must have hundreds of pictures of us by now."

"Look at them." Zander points, "Most of these are posed photographs by real photographers. Some look better than what we get on our phones."

"Here's one of us in front of the ship when we first went ashore at Amber Cove," Garret points out.

There are hundreds of photos on many partitions in the store. "It will take forever to find one of a cruise ship," Lexi says.

"Wait a minute," Zander says, "I don't see any of a cruise ship alone. Garret pull our picture and look at the back of it."

Garret pulls the picture off the wall and turns it over.

"Holy crap," Garret says with astonishment, "this is it. The clue. This was easy."

On the back of the photo is:

½ of Christopher Columbus plus 258
Enter with key
Take rosary
Hang rosary on bathroom mirror in your room

After they all look at it, Zander says, "Not so easy anymore."

Talin remembering the success she had with the clerk in the Art Gallery, says, "I'll take over." She takes the photo and goes to the Photo Gallery clerk.

Talin shows it to the lady, who is young and pretty, and says, "We found this."

"Fantastical!" the lady responds and taking the photo looks the four of them over. Looking directly at Zander she asks, "What do you say?"

Zander is dumbfounded. "What do you mean?"

The lady still holding the photo responds, "I'm from Italy, so I've got to hear you say it to me."

"Say what?" Zander asks.

There's a silence, then Garret catches on. "Tell her the code, Zander, tell her the code."

Zander remains silent.

The clerk smiling at Zander says, "Come on big boy, you can do it. Sei carino."

"What?"

"Sei carino, you're cute." She repeats in English.

"Say it, Zander, say it," the other three all say together.

Looking at his shoes Zander softly says, "Ahh, … I love you?

"What, I didn't hear you."

Bracing himself, Zander looks at her and repeats louder, "I love you," and then blushes. The other three are laughing as is the counter lady.

"Here," she says, "this is yours, free," and gives Zander a peck on the check as she hands him the photo. Zander is really blushing now.

Garret asks her, "Is there anything more you can tell us about this photo?"

"No, I've done my job; the rest is up to you. Buona fortunal."

"What does that mean?"

"Good luck."

They leave the photo shop happy about a quick find of the answer to the cipher clue, but perplexed about the new clue. How can they get lucky again? Walking slowly they discuss the new clue. Nobody has any idea of how to proceed with the new clue or who to ask for help.

Sadly Garret says, "This looks like the end to the scavenger hunt."

As they are walking by the casino, Lexi spots a quarter on the floor. It's by an unoccupied row of slot machines next to the walkway. She picks it up and looks at the slot machine with a sneaky look on her face.

"Lexi, what are you going to do?"

"I'm going to play the slot machine."

"Ah, Lexi you can't. You're too young to do that."

"There's nobody around. Watch me." Lexi quickly drops the quarter into the machine. "What do I do now? There's no lever; just a lot of buttons. Which one should I push?"

"How about the one that says 'play'," instructs Zander while looking around for any official that might arrest them or blacklist them from future cruises.

Lexi hits play and they watch symbols spin on reels behind five little windows. One reel stops, then another and another until all stop spinning. There's a pause and then the machine lights up and gives off a loud series of dings and dongs.

"What happened?" Lexi says excitedly, thinking that whatever it is, it is good.

"You won!" the others say in amazement. Zander looks around again. While people are noticing; they don't seem concerned about four kids around a slot machine. *Good.*

The machine flashes '$100.00 winner'. "I won $100.00," shouts Lexi, "OMG, What do I do now?"

"Be quiet," warns Zander.

Garret, after studying the face of the machine sees a button marked 'cash out' and presses it. A long white slip of paper is ejected from the machine. Lexi grabs it and reads $100.00. She about to go freaking crazy, but Zander pulls her away and tells her to shush. "There's a man in a white shirt with a name tag coming our way. Let's get out of here."

The kids run dodging around people in the crowded hallway. Zander is leading and to be safe, runs up two flights of stairs. They stop and watch down the steps. They are unaware that they are now on deck 7, the level they've always avoided. No one, who looks like an official or cruise person has followed.

"We're clear," Garret declares.

Lexi is jumping up and down. "OMG, I won $100.00! Awesome."

"What do you mean 'you'? We did this together," says Garret.

"Yeah, Lexi, we share it." Talin adds.

Lexi, disappointed she can't keep it all for herself agrees, "Yes, we share it."

"What are we going to do with it? We can't cash it in, we're too young. If we tell our parents, they'll probably just add it in our college funds. I'd like to use the money," says Zander.

"Me too." The others agree.

"Okay, let's just hold it until we figure out what to do," says Lexi and then realizing she doesn't have anywhere to put it, says, "I don't have any pockets."

"I do," says Zander and Lexi hands the slip of paper to him.

Before putting it away, Zander and the others examine the valuable paper. Then out of nowhere, the paper is snatched out of Zander's hand.

Chapter 22 The Robbery

It's Burt and he's alone. He reads the slip of paper and says, "Well, what do we have here? Looks like $100.00. I can get a really good tattoo now."

"That's not yours, give it back!" all the kids demand.

Burt takes a defiant stance, puts the paper in his pocket and says, "Who wants to try to get it?" Burt puts up his fists. "I can take all of you on."

"BURT, YOU'RE A BULLY!" Talin shouts.

"Talin, that doesn't help," Zander says calmly.

Zander then tries to reason with Burt and in a confident tone says, "Burt, I'd rather be friends than fight you. Why can't we be friends?" Zander again stands as tall as he can and stares Burt in the eyes. Zander is hoping Burt is still keeping his promise not to throw the first punch.

Burt lowers his fists and is quiet for awhile. Then Burt says, "Tell you what. My uncle just gave me my allowance, so I can get the tattoo. I'll give back the $100.00 if you fight me. Zander, you don't have to win the fight; you just have to fight me. Okay?"

Zander is quiet, not sure how to reply. His offer of friendship isn't working. Burt goes on, "We'll do it at the back end of the boat on deck 11. There's usually nobody around, just some fat guy who's always alone and usually playing on his Ipad. Pick a time."

"I still don't want a fight," Zander replies. "Can't we forget about it?"

"Pick a time tomorrow," Burt again demands, "I'm getting tired of waiting." With no response, Burt adds, "Okay, I'll pick the time. 9 o'clock tomorrow night. If you don't show up, you don't get the $100.00 back. And wimp, like you, I'm a man of my word."

"No, you're a bully!" Talin states again and getting really mad, she kicks Burt in the shin. It really hurt. Talin that is. Burt doesn't move or react. He just smiles and says, "Thanks little wimp, that felt good. Do it again and you'll regret it."

Lexi pulls a pissed off Talin away from Burt. Talin nurses her sore toe.

Zander, appearing to have an idea, says in a new confident way, "Okay Burt, 9 o'clock tomorrow night. Deck 11 at the stern of the boat. And you've got to bring Bernie and Brian with you."

Burt pauses before responding, "Ah, is stern the back of the boat?"

"Yes," Zander answers while the others chuckle to themselves. Burt isn't very smart.

"Good wimp, I'll see you there. Not sure if Bernie can make it, but Brian will be there." Burt looks at Garret. "You better be there too. Brian might want some action." Garret gives an uncaring reply, "Whatever."

Burt doesn't like that reply. Finally he walks away almost skipping in joy.

Garret is shocked, "Zander do you have a plan? You'll get hurt badly if you fight Burt."

"I have several plans," Zander answers, "First; he said I had to show up to get the $100.00. You heard him, right? I get the $100.00 from him first, and then run."

"Yeah," Garret replies, "but I don't think Burt will agree to that interpretation. I wouldn't rely entirely on that plan. Got another?"

"Second," Zander continues, "if Bernie's there, we get her to tell her father that Burt is in a fight."

Garret, "That's a little better, but Burt said Bernie might not be there which means he's not going to tell her."

"We'll tell her, which means we've got to find Bernie tomorrow."

"But Zander, even if Bernie is there, by the time she goes to get her father, you will have already been beaten up."

"That means we have to stall, but I've got one final idea which is the best one," and after Zander tells them his plan, Talin says "I can't do that!"

The kids decide to call it a night and go back to their rooms. The kids are not in a good mood. $100.00 was stolen from them, and Zander has to fight Burt. Tomorrow is going to be a dreadful day, and grandpa is certain to ask again if they're having a good time.

Chapter 23 La Romano, Dominican Republic

DAY 5

After breakfast and homework, it's time to go on the excursion. We leave the ship and with other cruise passengers get into the back of a two ton truck that goes to a beach near the town of La Romano. La Romano is the place where Burt thinks he can get a tattoo. *I hope it hurts or causes an infection so bad he can't fight me.* Zander is thinking.

The road out of town becomes a single lane of sand and gravel through the jungle. It is extremely rough riding with lots of pot holes. There are small open fields with fencing. The fence posts are tree limbs. Barbed wire is strung from post to post. The few animals are cows, goats, horses and donkeys. There are donkeys with packs being pulled along the road by the locals. Our truck has to stop to wait for some Dominicans to prod and pull a big pig across the road. Our guide says they are going to slaughter and butcher the pig on the other side of the road. The other side of the road has no buildings, so it must be an open air butcher shop!

The road goes by many houses that are small and many look more like a shack than a house. There are air conditioners in some windows, so people must live in them. There are very few cars, but a lot of scooters the people use for travel. There are a few banana plantations which do have some nice homes. The locals probably refer to them as mansions, but to the kids, they are just old, regular houses.

At the beach, a trio of old men are making music beating on pots and pans. There's a bucket in front of them for donations. There are several tables of homemade baskets, straw hats, wood carvings, etc. Women stand behind the tables in colorful dresses begging somebody to buy something.

"Grandpa," Lexi asks, "are these people poor?"

"Yes, out here in the countryside, the people are poor. However in the bigger cities in the Dominican Republic there are sewers, water, schools, hospitals, modern buildings and so on. In the countryside, the only public service they have is electricity and it's unreliable."

"Would Chile be the same?" Lexi is thinking of Diego.

"Some parts of Chile would be, yes, particularly in the countryside."

The kids change into swim suits and grab some snorkeling gear. Other trucks keep delivering cruise passengers to the beach, but Bernie is not among them. The kids have a good time swimming in the salt water and trying to stand against the powerful waves without falling down. They see colorful fish with the snorkeling masts on and learn that the fish will eat almost anything out of their hand.

During lunch, grandpa notices the kids not clowning around like they usually do. Instead they appear to be having a serious conversation and Zander is looking depressed. Something seems to be bothering him.

So grandpa intervenes with what he thinks would be interesting information. He begins with, "Are you having a good time?" Without waiting for an answer he continues, "Did you know the Dominican Republic is where Christopher Columbus first landed in 1492? Most people think it was America when he discovered the new world, but no, it was the Dominican Republic." The kids are quiet and respectful. They don't tell grandpa he's repeating what he told them in Amber Cove.

Undeterred, grandpa goes on, "This Island of the Dominican Republic is divided into two countries. The other country is ...."

"Haiti." Zander interrupts. "We know grandpa."

Since the kids don't seem interested, grandpa announces he's going to find some shade and take his nap. The kids are relieved.

Before he departs, Garret asks him, "Grandpa, do you know what ½ Christopher Columbus means?"

"No I don't. Why do you ask?"

"It's on the last clue we found."

"Could be only his first or only his last name. Otherwise, I have no idea."

After lunch the kids study a picture board with all the different fish they might see while snorkeling. They recognize the angelfish, clown fish and trumpet fish that they saw.

"Some look like the fish we have in the aquarium at home," says Garret.

"But these are a lot bigger," adds Zander.

They want to find a starfish and a lionfish. The counter lady directs them to a part of the beach where there's a coral reef and the best viewing this time of day.

"Are there any sharks?" Talin asks.

"Oh you might see a little one," the counter lady replies, "but it's rare."

That's all Talin needs to hear to decide to stay near her parents who are reading while sitting in lounge chairs at the edge of the beach, except her dad. He's getting a foot massage for 25 cents from a local native.

Chapter 24 Shops

After the day at the beach, it's another bumpy truck ride back to the ship. The truck however doesn't drop us off at the pier but several blocks away. The kids are tired and wonder why they have to walk so far to get back to the ship. Grandpa believes it's part of a plan to get tourists to buy something in the shops which line the path back to the ship.

The buildings are old and the people working in them stand in doorways begging for customers. "Come in. Look at my shop." "For you I give special deal." "I have something you need."

There are shops selling straw hats and baskets. Others sell seashells, jewelry, rum, ceramics, wood carvings and so on.

The women go into a couple clothing/souvenir shops and grandpa after examining some of the items says, "Some of these things are made in China." In fact one of the t-shirts Lexi's mom buys for her has the 'Made in China' label.

Again Talin's parents have to vouch for her in order to board the ship. The kids change quickly into evening clothes and get permission to walk around the ship before dinner.

They have three missions: find Bernie, Tank and solve the Columbus clue.

They wander the hallways and go up to Deck 11. Tank is not there. "Maybe he'll be at dinner tonight," says Talin.

"I hope so," replies Zander, "Now, how do we find Bernie? We don't even know her room number."

"I know it," Talin says, "She told me it's 710."

Zander snarls back at her, "Why didn't you say so before?"

"I thought we agreed to stay away from the deck 7. Look what happened the last time we were on the deck 7." Talin is upset.

"We don't go to her room; we call her on the room phone."

"Oh," now Talin is really upset and twirls her hair.

They go to Zander's room and Zander dials room 710. Fortunately, Bernie answers. Zander explains to Bernie what is set to happen at 9 o'clock tonight. Bernie says she'll tell her dad and he'll stop it. Zander tells her not to. Such a move won't stop Burt; he'll just get madder, set another time or plan an ambush. This thing won't be over. He has another plan but needs Bernie there. Bernie says she'll try to be there if she can get away from her parents.

Meanwhile, Garret is thinking numbers. ½ Christopher Columbus has to be a number because the clue says add 258. You can only add a number to another number. Then the clue says enter with key, so that must mean a room number. What number could be associated with Christopher Columbus? Okay Garret is thinking Columbus discovered America in 1492. One half of 1492 is 746. 746 plus 258 is 1004. We're on deck 10.

Garret leaves the room and walks down the hallway, and holy cow, there's a room 1004! Garret reads the sign on room 1004. UNBELIEVABLE! Garret runs back to tell the others what he found.

Chapter 25 The Rosary

"Listen everyone; I think I've solved the Christopher Columbus clue. Come with me."

While they follow Garret, he explains how he came up with the number 1004. They get to room 1004 and are amazed to see the sign on the door that reads, ROOM STEWARD.

"Now what?" asks Zander, "The clue says 'enter with key'."

"So who's got the key? We have to ask Diego and I'm not doing that." Lexi says.

As they are standing there, Garret tries to turn the door knob. It's locked.

They are about to return to their rooms when Garret says, "Wait, let me try something. The clue doesn't say anything about finding a key. That might mean we already have it." Garret takes out his Ship and Sail card and enters it into the key slot. The light on the door knob turns green!

"It's a universal lock. Maybe any key card will open it." Garret is excited. He opens the door and inside they see shelves of linen, towels, bath supplies and so on.

"The universal lock is so anybody can get a replacement of something in case the room steward isn't here." Although Garret is guessing, he is talking like he knows these things.

"Okay," Lexi says, "the next line in the clue is 'take rosary'. What's a rosary?"

"It's right there," Zander says and points to rosary beads hanging on the opposite wall.

Lexi quickly grabs them and says, "Let's leave before Diego comes. We have to hang these on the bathroom mirror."

They go back to their rooms and Lexi, not understanding why, hangs the rosary beads.

Then Lexi says to the others, "Hey, this time we didn't find a clue, right? Maybe we're at the end?"

Garret, scratching his head, observes, "If we're at the end, what did we get? A set of rosary beads! No, I think the rosary beads are another clue. The hardest clue so far. Lexi, is there anything written anywhere on the beads?"

Lexi retrieves the beads, examines them and finds faintly engraved letters on the back of the cross. The letters are hard to read, but she concludes they say 'Diego'.

Now Talin gets nervous, "We have to give them back. They belong to Diego. Think how mad he can get."

"Oh, we'll give then back, of course." Zander says, "The clue said to take them; that's our defense."

"I hope Diego is aware of the clue." Garret says.

"I think Diego has been behind this scavenger hunt all along," Lexi says.

"For instance, he knew we needed to translate the French clue and then that book shows up. Plus, it disappeared from my room when we went to the beach yesterday. Grandpa was with us and never had an opportunity to enter our room when we weren't here."

"La, la, la," Talin adds, "grandpa doesn't have a key to our room, either, duh."

"Okay, it's agreed," Garret summarizes, "we keep the beads because we believe Diego is responsible for the scavenger hunt. Next time we see him we give him the beads and see what happens. I wonder why we were to hang them on the mirror?"

"So Diego can easily find them when he tidies up our room tonight," Lexi says triumphantly.

Zander isn't listening. He's preoccupied with tonight's events.

The parents tell the kids it's time to go to dinner.

9:00 p.m. is getting closer.

Chapter 26 Zander has a Date

At dinner the kids plead for their own table again. Grandma suggests we should all eat together at a table for 10 because the dining room doesn't look crowded. The maître de has a table for 10 immediately available, so grandma wins.

In the middle of the large table for 10 is an ice sculpture of a swan. The adults talk about the sculpture. The kids look for Tank. If he's here, he should be easy to spot because our table is on a higher level than the rest of the restaurant.

Talin pretends she is a queen reigning over her subjects on the lower level.

"There he is!" Zander exclaims.

"Who?" his mother asks, surprised by Zander's sudden outburst.

Suspiciously calm now, Zander answers, "Oh, just somebody we've met. Talin, why don't you go over and tell him hi for us."

"I don't see him," Talin responds.

Lexi, "How can you miss him; he's so big. Over there," and Lexi points.

"Somebody come with me." Talin pleads.

"I will," Zander volunteers. After all, it's Zander's plan.

When Zander and Talin return, Zander gives an 'it's all arranged nod' to Lexi and Garret.

Grandpa then says, "Isn't that the same guy that bought you a drink the first night in here, Talin?"

"Yes, grandpa."

"So you're friends now?"

"Yes, grandpa." Talin says again, hoping this is the end of the questions.

Well, it would have been if that same Pilipino waiter 'Don" hadn't brought 4 banana bonkers for the kids. The waiter is about to leave…

"Wait a minute," grandpa demands, "who's paying for those?"

The waiter looks at Talin and she nods, okay. "The large gentleman over in the far corner. The one by himself and playing on his Ipad."

Oh crud, the kids think. Now the questions will come. The kids handle the grilling well. They explain how they helped him get out of a broken chair last night. Talin and Zander went over to see how he was feeling tonight. The drinks are thanks for their helping him. All the answers of the kids are true. *There are no questions about tonight's plans until midway through dinner.*

"You kids will enjoy tonight's show at the theater. It features juggling and acrobatics!" one of the parents says.

"What time is the show?" Zander asks.

"7:30."

"When will it get over?"

"I don't know, probably a little after 9."

Zander is freaked out. *What to do?*

Zander tries getting out of the going to the show. He tries, "it'll be boring", "I don't like the theater"; "I'm not feeling well"; and finally, "please don't make me."

To the adults it definitely sounds like Zander is hiding something and he's digging his hole deeper.

Then grandpa comes unknowingly to his rescue, "I know what it is…"

Zander and the kids are stunned, *how does grandpa know?*

"…. he's meeting a girl, obviously," and grandpa sits there smiling at Zander.

Now, all the adults are stunned by the grandpa's suggestion, but Zander is after all, a teenager now, having recently turned thirteen.

Zander thinks he smells an opportunity and admits, "Yes, I've made plans to meet a girl at the teen club at 9 o'clock. So, if I have to go to the show, can I at least leave early, say 8:30?"

There's a moment of silence during which Zander's parents are sort of choking and each take a drink of water. Garret and Lexi are looking wide eyed with mouths open at Zander. Talin completes Zander ruse by saying, "I knew it. He did ask that girl. She's cute." Talin takes it further by acting with a smirk and victory circle of her head.

Grandpa, thinking for some unknown reason he has a handle on things of the heart says, "8:30, I suggest he doesn't have to go to the show at all, if he doesn't want too. He's so nervous he won't see or remember anything at the show. This is a big event for a boy at 13. Even at noon today I saw that something was really bothering him. This explains everything."

If you only knew everything, thinks Zander.

Grandma tells grandpa to stay out of it. This is a decision for the parents.

"You go to the show with the rest of us, but you can leave at 8:30," say his parents.

"Me too," Garret chips in.

"You got a date too?" his parents ask.

Blushing, Garret replies, "No, but I can be his wing man."

"Do you even know what a wing man does?"

Before Garret can think of an answer, Lexi says, "I'll be the chaperone.'

Talin, "If they all go, I get to go."

Okay, all the parents surrender and agree that the kids can leave the show at 8:30. But a question remains in their minds: they haven't seen any girls Zander's age on the ship.

Chapter 27 The Showdown

9:00 p.m. Deck 11

The four kids arrive at the deck 11 stern. Tank is there, sitting on what appears to be a stronger chair than he had before and playing on his Ipad. Nobody else is present.

"Thanks for coming," Zander says to Tank.

"No problem, good luck," he replies. He puts his chair back and pretends to go to sleep.

Brian arrives and looks around. He smiles at Lexi and says "Hi Lexi". She smiles and says Hi back. He makes a motion, and Burt comes up the stairs.

"Just making sure there's no surprise ambush," Burt says.

Geez, Garret is thinking; *this guy is military all the way.*

"Okay let's get this started." Burt raises his fists, then looks over at Garret and says to him, "Garret, Brian says he won't fight you, so after I'm done with Zander, you're next."

Now I know what a wing man is for. Garret is thinking.

"Wait," Zander says, "Give me the $100.00 casino slip first. I showed up, didn't I?"

"No way, wimp. You have to fight me first."

There's goes plan number one.

Burt approaches Zander and before he speaks again, Bernie comes running up the steps and onto the deck. "Hi Talin. Am I too late?"

Plan number 2 is now in play.

"Bernie, why are you here? This has nothing to do with you." Burt says angrily. Then to Zander, "You did this. Can't you fight your own battles without a little tattletale girl to squeal on me?"

Bernie speaks up, "Burt, you know I'll tell my dad if you're in a fight. You won't get your allowance next week."

"I can go without my allowance next week. I'm too much in need of some physical action **right now**!" and does some jabs in the air like he's warming up.

There's goes plan number two, Garret thinks.

"I'm going to go get my dad," Bernie says and she heads for the steps.

"Go ahead; this will be over before he gets here," says Burt while skipping like a boxer, moving closer to Zander who in turn is backing up closer to Tank.

Oh oh, plan number 3 doesn't look too good right now.

Zander backs up closer to Tank who now appears to be sleeping.

Burt keeps jabbing into the air and doing little skips. He's still warming up. Zander decides to keep his arms limp at his sides. He doesn't want to give any indication that he's going to participate in a battle.

110

"Burt," Zander makes another plea, "I don't want to do this. Can I just have the $100.00, be friends and we call this off?" Zander moves to the side and keeps moving in a circle while facing Burt. Now Burt and Zander are both equal distance from Tank who now sounds like he's snoring.

Garret hears Tank snoring and thinks, *Plan number four may be down the toilet. But plan number three is still in play, if Zander can keep Burt talking instead of fighting.*

"Zander, I bet you play sports at school?" Burt asks.

"Yes, baseball," then Zander decides to exaggerate. *Maybe more sports will cause Burt to think I'm stronger than he thinks.* "I also play football, soccer, basketball, roller hockey and I wakeboard and water-ski."

How about that, my brother is an All American.

"Good, that makes you a better challenge for me. I particularly like beating up football players. Glad to hear you're one."

Nice try, Zander, but it didn't work.

"What sports do you play?" Zander asks while moving further sideways in the circle, but still facing Burt directly. This causes Burt to move so he can stay faced directly across from Zander. The snoring Tank is behind Burt now.

"I don't play any. I used to, but any time I got on a team, the army relocates my dad and we have to move. Then at the new school the team players have already been picked and I can't join. Couldn't become their friends then either. That all sucked. So fighting, boxing and martial arts are my sports now. You don't need a team to do those things."

Too bad he didn't pick fishing or golf.

Zander, while distracting Burt by asking him questions, moves closer to Burt, causing Burt to unknowingly back up, "What about weight lifting? Do you do that too? You look strong."

Compliment the opponent, buys time, keep it up Zander.

"Enough talk," yells Burt, who has become impatient, "throw the first punch, **now!"**

Whoops, the stall plan is over.

Zander moves closer, Burt backs up a little. Zander's hands are still at his sides.

"My promise not to throw the first punch is over. I give you 5 seconds before I do. 5, 4, 3,…**UGH**".

Chapter 28 The Rescue

Burt has been pulled down on top of Tank by Tank. Tank uses Burt like a crutch to get out of the chair in order to stand. He has Burt by a big grab of the back of Burt's shirt. He turns Burt around with his other large hand and grabs the front of Burt's shirt. He releases the back of the shirt.

Holding Burt at arm's length, Tank waddles towards the wall and pins Burt against it.

"What are you doing? Let me go, fat man!" Burt demands.

Burt struggles to free himself. There's no way he can escape unless his shirt tears from Tank's grip. If he does escape, there's no way Tank can catch him.

Tank talks calmly and quietly, "I'm not a fat man, I'm a whale." He winks and smiles at Talin. Talin returns the smile and curtsies.

Burt is really mad, "If you hit me, I'll sue the pants off of you!"

"Pants off, that's a good idea" Tank replies, "I'll not hit you. Instead I'll take all your clothes off and throw them in the ocean…unless you promise to leave these friends of mine alone," and Tank smiles at him.

This scares Burt more than getting beaten. He doesn't mind being naked, but he can't have Bernie, her father or his mother see the tattoo on his butt. His father would then find out!

Burt decides to fight back. He kicks Tank in the lower abdomen, over and over. Tank raises him up so that

Burt's feet leave the ground and he presses Burt harder against the wall. This doesn't stop the kicking by Burt.

Tank tries to stop the kicking with his other hand. Before he gets Burt's kicking under control, Burt lands a hard kick to Tank's groin. Tank gives out a groan and grimaces in pain. He moves his hand from the shirt to Burt's throat, presses hard, choking Burt. He gives Burt the look of a real mad man. Anger is written all over Tank's face. Burt is freaked by the change in Tank. Burt is now scared and he pees his pants.

"Okay, I give," Burt barely gets the words out. Tank loosens his grip and in a deep angry voice says, "What did you say?"

"I give up. Let me down. I won't bother Zander and his friends. I'll give the $100.00 back. I promise. Just let me down....please."

Tank appears to be in pain. He remains silent and doesn't release Burt.

Now in a panic, Burt pulls the $100.00 casino paper out of his pants pocket. "Zander, here's the $100.00; take it. Call this beast off of me."

Zander grabs the $100.00, and then Tank slowly releases Burt.

Talin runs up to Tank, "Are you okay?"

Tank slowly makes his way to his chair in a stooped position. Talin gives him support. While her help is useless, Tank pretends to use it and sits down. "Thank you, Talin; I'm okay. I just need to rest a little. You can go on your way."

Meanwhile, Burt adjusts his clothes and silently with his head down and hands in front of his pants, starts walking to the stairway. He notices Brian hasn't joined him. "Brian, are you coming?"

Brian looks over at Lexi who smiles back, "No, Burt; you go ahead. You're just going to sulk in your room. I'll find something to do on my own."

Bernie comes up from the stairwell. "Is your dad coming?" Burt asks her.

"No, I never went to get him. I stayed here watching everything from the upper steps."

"Are you going to tell him?"

"No, I see no need. You know you were a jerk tonight," as Bernie looks at the front of Burt's pants and laughs.

Burt, dejected and humiliated, goes down the steps.

Zander thanks Tank for coming to his rescue. "When I heard you snoring, I was worried that you really were asleep."

Tank grins, "I wasn't. The snoring was my idea."

The four kids plus Brian, Bernie and Tank talk about and rehash what just happened. Zander didn't have to fight; they got the $100.00 back; Burt was humiliated; and no parents were involved. Talin again asks if he is okay. Tank appears to be in less pain now and says he'll be fine.

"Listen, kids," Tank says, "there are two things I want to tell you. First, how to handle a bully. I've had lots of experience."

"Zander, you did it perfectly. You showed confidence and strength and that you weren't afraid without being threatening. Bullies want to intimidate but you weren't letting him intimidate you. Being cool and confident with a bully makes them uncomfortable and that maybe their behavior is wrong."

"But the best part is you asking him to be a friend. People usually become bullies because they either don't have friends or low self esteem. Picking on others makes them feel good. Offering friendship shows them a better way to feel good.

"I think, no matter what, he was going to fight," Zander says.

"I agree and that's why having an adult around as a last resort is the best way to tame a bully. I'm glad to be the one. Lord knows I've faced enough bullies when I was a kid. This was payback. Give him some discipline he obviously hasn't otherwise been getting. It teaches respect."

"Now here's what I expect will happen. He'll keep his word not to bother you again. In fact he may even offer his friendship."

"I think he will too," offers Brian, standing next to Lexi.

Zander feeling relieved, says to Tank, "You said you had two things to tell us."

Tank picks up his Ipad, acts as if he just had a sudden pain and says in a struggling voice, "Yes. Don't become addicted to video games." He puts his head back and closes his eyes.

"Are you okay? Do you want us to go get help?" Talin asks.

Tank opens his eyes and replies, "Why thank you for the offer, Talin. I rarely receive such attention. And I thank all of you for letting me be part of the action tonight. I feel like I did something useful for a change. No, Talin I don't need help. I'll sit awhile and think about the fun I had tonight. Then call it a night and go to my room."

The kids depart but are bothered by his words. It didn't seem like he was feeling well.

Chapter 29 The Reward

"Let's celebrate," suggests Bernie, "the Motown Band is playing in the Atrium Lounge and I have to meet my parents there anyway." "Okay," the others say. Talin and Bernie lead the way.

All the parents and grandparents are at the Atrium Lounge together at a table close to the dance floor. It's crowded, but the kids plus Brian and Bernie, find a table in the back. The kids make their presence known and arrangements are made for six banana bonkers. Zander is, of course, asked about his date and tells them she didn't show up.

"Oh that's too bad; you got stood up."

"No, I'm good," Zander replies.

Lexi's parents kid Zander's parents about it, until Zander's parents point to the dance floor. They see Lexi dancing with some boy!

At the kids table, Talin and Bernie are singing the songs being played by the Motown Band even though they hardly know the words. Zander is relieved the evening's confrontation is over and enjoying his drink. Garret enjoys watching the antics of the band even though the music is before his time. Lexi and Brian remain on the dance floor under the ever watchful eyes of her parents.

It soon becomes time for everybody to return to their rooms. Upon returning to her room, Lexi immediately looks for the rosary beads and **they are gone!**

Moments later, there's a knock on her door and also a knock on the doors of everybody else. Everyone goes into the hallway. Diego is there with a big grin on his face.

"Sorry to bother you at this late time. I have important announcement. In all my years as room steward, nobody has completed my scavenger hunt. I present to each of you kids a cruise ship shirt." Diego is beaming and hands out the shirts.

"So it was you," says Lexi. "I thought so. But how did you know we were solving the clues?"

"By finding solved clues in your waste baskets."

"The rosary was the last one?" Zander asks.

"Si. I would have awarded you each your own rosary beads, but the higher ups said I shouldn't do that."

"The shirts are fine," says Garret, "Thank you."

"Oh, but that not all." Diego continues excitedly, "You get behind-the-scenes ship tour by me personally. It's better than the one they sell for $125.00. You'll see the bridge, huge kitchens, engine room, deck where cruise people live and so on. Can we do it tomorrow morning at 10 am? It will take only hour."

Grandpa gets excited, "can we all go?'

Diego responds, "You did the scavenger hunt too?"

"Umm, no."

"Sorry, higher ups let me do this on condition that it be limited to only those who solve puzzle. We always expected two people, but in this case permission granted for four. I don't want to try to make it more. I guess it's because there is a behind-the-scenes ship tour you can buy."

Chapter 30 Ship Tour

DAY 6

The next morning after completing their homework, the kids go with Diego on his behind-the-scenes ship tour. They are wearing their new cruise shirts. They go on the bridge where the captain steers the ship and controls the engines. They meet the captain who tells them about the side thrusters. The kids remain respectfully silent and don't mention that they already knew about the thrusters from grandpa.

Next are the crew quarters which are rooms similar to the passengers' staterooms but smaller. There are stores, beauty shop, dining mess, crew bar and a gym for only the crew. They learn about the ship's water supply, electrical power and waste disposal. There are huge laundry, storage and garbage rooms.

Talin is most interested in the backstage area for the theater with its changing rooms, prop storage area and lighting controls. Zander thinks the mooring room is interesting with huge tie lines and dock bumpers, each as big as his family's ski boat. Garret is most entertained by the water cannons and sonic horns that can be used to repel a pirate attack.

"Are there really pirate attacks anymore?" he asks.

"Oh yes," Diego explains, "if we cruise near the shores of a poor and troubled country there's always the risk of desperate people threatening a cruise ship and its passengers in return for money. Especially if there's no navy ships close by. The water cannons get attached to high pressure hoses which can knock a pirate over. The acoustic horns emit an ear splitting sound that makes a person cover their ears so they can't use their hands to hold a gun or climb the railing. You don't hear about these things because the cruise lines don't want the bad publicity. It would be bad for business."

Lexi, however, is more into finding out about Diego. She learns, like all of the crew, he works long hours for low pay. He might be on the ship for up to six months straight with rarely a day off. He sees his family only twice a year. There are crew members from over 30 countries, but none from the United States. The reason is that the pay is lower and the hours longer than U. S. citizens are willing to accept.

Lexi concludes Diego might be poor. She asks Diego if he is from a countryside area in Chile. He is.

"Are the people poor where you are from?"

"Yes. Some don't have inside plumbing. Few have full-time jobs. The school is open-air building. Electricity works only part of time. There are few cars. People get around on buses that break down a lot. Chickens, dogs and goats run in the dirt streets. Does that paint a picture for you?"

Oh, oh, Diego is getting upset again.

Lexi decides to change the subject, "What about people who get sick on the ship?"

Diego isn't done, "I, however, have job, as much as I hate it. I send money home and my family lives well, though I am rarely there to enjoy life with them. We have a TV with satellite dish. Neighbors come to my house to watch TV. We have a car. So we are more fortunate than others, but not as fortunate as people in United States.

Lexi, be thankful for what you have. Enough lecture, let me show you the medical facility."

Thank goodness, I hope he's done.

On the way to the ship's medical center, they pass the brig where people who cause trouble are jailed. "Mostly drunks" Diego adds. Then a morgue where up to six bodies can be stored until the ship reaches port.

Garret asks, "Do people die often on the ship?"

"Considering that most passengers are old people, yes, it's common."

All the kids agree there were a lot of old people on this trip.

They reach the medical center which is impressive. Almost like a small hospital with two intensive care rooms, examining tables, and a lot of white machines. A doctor from India greets them and shows them around. A curtain surrounds one of the intensive care units. Diego notices and says, "So you have patient today?"

"Yes," the Indian doctor replies in perfect English, "an unusual one. The biggest man I've ever seen. Came in last night."

Chapter 31 Medical Center

"TANK!' Talin shouts, "It must be Tank." Talin is freaking.

"Can we see him?" Zander asks.

"I'm afraid not. He didn't put any names on the permitted visitor list."

A disappointed look is on all of the kids' faces.

The doctor is surprised by the kids' reactions, so he continues, "He said he is alone on this trip, and his name is not Tank. His name is… what was it, o yes, Erwin."

"Erwin is Tank's real name. We need to see him," says Talin.

Just then, a voice is barely heard from the other side of the curtain, "Doctor, let them in; it's okay; they are my friends."

The doctor pulls aside the curtain and there is Tank lying on a hospital bed that is too small for him. There are various tubes and lines attached to his body. His face has been shaved and his hair cut short. His face looks different, definitely better, but he is easily recognizable by his stomach, which looks like a mountain from Talin's level on the floor.

Talin requests a chair to stand on and the doctor provides one. She sees an Ipad resting on his stomach.

"Hi Talin," Tank says, "How are you?"

"I'm fine, how are you?" There are tears in Talin's eyes.

"I'll be okay."

Lexi interjects with, "I've heard you say that too many times. You're not okay; look at you and all this stuff."

"Burt caused this, didn't he?" Zander asks.

"Not really. The doctor says stress and being overweight is the real cause. Actually it is a blessing. This good doctor behind you is from India and his specialty is obesity. Did you know there are a lot of extremely fat people in India?"

"No. I didn't."

"They from the US", Diego interrupts, "so naturally they don't know much about other countries."

Please Diego; give it a rest, Lexi is thinking.

"Anyway," continues Tank, "this doctor knows of a procedure that is done in India that can fix the type of obesity I have. It's still experimental in the United States, which is why I haven't had it. So after I get home and rest up, I'm going to India to become a normal human being. I can't wait. If it hadn't been for you kids and that awful Burt, I wouldn't have had this opportunity."

"Tank, if you hadn't been there last night, I might have been the one on this table," Zander says and then adds, "Again, thank you very much."

"Zander, again I tell you that you handled that bully very well. You didn't show any weakness, stayed firm and unfazed. He couldn't get into your head. That's why he took so long to begin the fight. But, hey, anything for my friend, Talin. She helped me on the plane with my shoes and she makes me laugh." Tank coughs.

Talin says, "Maybe you'll be on the same plane with us when we fly back to Chicago? I can help you with your shoes again."

"No, I may be bed ridden for awhile before I can fly back to Chicago. You go ahead without me and you can have my seat." Tank thinks he made a joke and starts with a bad coughing spell.

The doctor says the kids should leave now. However, before they are out of the room, Tank, now over the coughing, says "If you're in the dining room tonight, Dakila will bring you banana bonkers. I have a standing arrangement with him."

"Who's Dakila?" Garret asks.

"The Pilipino waiter." Tank answers.

"So that's why I got one the night you weren't in the dining room?" Talin asks.

"Yes, and he told me you liked the banana bonker better than the others."

The tour is over, the kids are sad and then Diego begins to speak.

Oh no, not another lecture about us dumb Americans, Lexi thinks.

"You kids are special. You are smart; you solved my scavenger hunt. You are compassionate; I saw that with the big guy. I am honored to be your room steward. I apologize for calling you dumb foreigners. The world is lucky to have people like you." Diego bows and starts to walk away.

"Wait," Lexi says, "just a minute," and she huddles with the other three.

Chapter 32 Outdoor Movie

Lexi walks up to Diego and hands him a crumpled piece of paper.

"What is this? A scavenger hunt for me?" Diego unfolds the paper. It's the $100.00 casino slip. "Wow, this is difficult clue."

"It's not a clue," Lexi says, "it's real. We won it but we can't cash it in; we're too young. We don't want to tell our parents about it. So we'd like you to have it. It's thanks for the scavenger hunt and giving us the tour today."

"Yeah, your scavenger hunt was much better than the ones our grandpa sets up for us," Garret says and then adds, "You said you would keep secrets from our parents."

"If it weren't for you, we wouldn't have seen Tank today," says Talin.

Diego is overcome. "Thank you. Again, I am honored to be your room steward. You are the best passengers I ever had." Diego walks away trying to hold back tears.

"What to do now?" Lexi asks.

"Swimming," the others agree and run to their rooms.

That night, dinner is again at the center table for 10, this time adorned with an ice sculpture of a sail fish.

Grandpa asks, "Are you having a good time?"

Again the kids say yes, but this time it's true.

The same Pilipino waiter delivers a banana bonker to each of the kids.

"Thank you, Dakila," they each say even though his name tag says 'Don'.

He looks surprised and smiles in appreciation. "I heard you are good kids and you had a visit with him today."

The adults are mystified. Grandpa asks the waiter, "Isn't Don your name? That's what your name tag says."

The waiter responds, "Don on name tag is for benefit of you from the States. It's easier than using my real name, Dakila."

Grandpa continues, "May I assume these drinks for the kids are not going on my tab?"

"Yes sir, you are correct," and the waiter leaves.

All the adults give the kids a puzzled look. They reply with one word, "Tank".

"Tell us about your behind the scenes ship tour today. Did you have a good time?" grandpa asks.

After dinner, the kids willingly agree to go to the show tonight which is a musical review. After the show the kids want to watch the outdoor movie which is a recent animated film on the big screen on deck 9. Permission is granted. The parents want to go to the comedy club which is for adults only anyway.

The grandkids go to the outdoor movie and meet the 3 Bs. Lexi sits with Brian and Talin sits with Bernie. Burt is quiet and hanging back. He has his hands in his pockets and is looking down at his shoes. He approaches slowly.

"Hi guys," he says softly. Zander and Garret each take a step back.

"Don't worry; I'm not going to touch you. I keep my word."

"What do you want?" Zander asks.

"Is the offer to be friends still open?"

"Could be," Zander responds, "what do you have in mind?"

"Maybe we could hang together. I haven't had many friends. One is my brother and since last night he doesn't talk to me. I think he's in love, actually."

The three of them look over at Lexi and Brian who are laughing, sharing a box of popcorn and watching the movie.

"All right," says Zander, "you can sit with us,"

They get popcorn and find a table.

"You guys outsmarted me last night. I was prepared in case you had a knife. Brought one with me just in case, but I never expected that big guy was involved. That was impressive."

Wow, think both Zander and Garret, *he had a knife!*

"You got one now?"

"No, I had taken it from the dining room. I've put it back."

Burt is silent, something is bothering him. Finally he says, "I use fear to get people to respect me. But Zander it didn't work with you. Guys, I apologize for the way I treated you."

Another period of silence and then Zander says "Apology accepted," and the three of them do fist bumps. The movie is of little interest to them as Burt tells them about army life and the many altercations he has had. He actually is quite entertaining.

Over by Talin, Bernie declares Talin as her BFF. Talin says ditto. They pledge never to twirl their hair again and exchange email addresses. Together they sing along with every song in the movie.

The movie ends and the kids go back to their rooms. Grandpa is there and naturally asks if they had a good time. But from their looks and actions, Grandpa can easily tell the answer is YES!

In their rooms, in addition to the usual towel made animal, there's a balloon.

On the bed there's no mint. Instead there's a box of mints!

DAY 7

The next morning the ship is already in the Fort Lauderdale Port. Everybody has to get off the ship by noon so the staterooms and the whole ship can be cleaned for next group of passengers arriving that afternoon. Fuel is being pumped into the ship. Garbage from the just completed cruise is being offloaded and crates of food and supplies are being loaded on board for the next cruise that leaves that same evening.

For the kids, it's a travel day. It's pack, disembark, take a shuttle to the airport, wait for the flight and fly to Chicago. It's a long day, but nobody minds. Each kid relives in their mind the memories of a wonderful cruising experience. Then its pick up luggage, take a shuttle to the parking garage and give kisses and hugs for grandpa and grandma.

Lastly, Grandpa asks one more time: Did you have a good time?

Acknowledgements

This book was inspired by a recent cruise and my four oldest grandchildren. While the grandchildren were not on the cruise, I wanted to give them the experience through a story.

Many thanks to my wife, Diane and family, including the grandchildren, whose reaction to the story caused me to publish for others to enjoy.

Also many thanks to Denny Corrigan, Jim Magee, Barbara L. Johnson and Larry and Karen Windsor for their suggestions, editing and encouragement.

About the author

Lawrence W. Baxter is a retired attorney in North Central Illinois. He has written numerous short stories of only family value. His law practice involved writing numerous briefs, memos, appeals, pleadings and contracts. He dislikes fantasy and science fiction, believing that fiction should be more than just entertaining. It should also be educational, plausible and realistic.

After retiring, completing the family genealogy, converting home movies to DVD's, playing video games and making hundreds of wire tree sculptures; he turned his attention to writing. Two more books are underway.

Made in the USA
Lexington, KY
13 April 2018